ROBERT BARNARD

Robert Barnard was born and brought up in
Essex. After reading English at Balliol College,
Oxford, he worked for a time for the Fabian
Society, and in 1961 went as a lecturer in
English to the University of New England, in
New South Wales. He taught in Norwegian
universities for seventeen years from 1966,
and in 1983 came back to Britain to write full
time. As well as nearly thirty mysteries, he
has written books on Dickens, Agatha Christie
and a history of English literature. He and his
wife now live in Leeds.

ROBERT BARNARD

Masters of the House

HarperCollins*Publishers*

HarperCollins*Publishers*
77–85 Fulham Palace Road,
Hammersmith, London W6 8JB

This paperback edition 1995
1 3 5 7 9 8 6 4 2

First published in Great Britain by
HarperCollins*Publishers* 1994

Copyright © Robert Barnard 1994

The Author asserts the moral right to
be identified as the author of this work

ISBN 0 00 649326 2

Set in Meridien and Bodoni

Printed in Great Britain by
HarperCollinsManufacturing Glasgow

CHAPTER 1

After the First Death

'No!' screamed the woman on the bed.

She had caught a gesture, the merest suspicion of a shaken head from the doctor as he handed the little scrap of a baby to the nurse to be put in the incubator. The doctor turned back to her, smiling encouragement.

'No!'

'There, there, Mrs – Heenan, isn't it? You must think of yourself now.'

'And of all your other children,' said the sister, who knew Mrs Heenan's family situation better than the obstetrician.

Mrs Heenan protested no more. She looked from one face to the other, as if anxious, even in the midst of her terrible pain, to assure herself of the import of their words. Then she gave a little sigh and closed her eyes. It was as if she had gently unslipped the boat she was lying in from its moorings, and was beginning the drift out to sea.

The obstetrician knew the signs. He leaned forward urgently.

'Mrs Heenan, it's important you get a grip on yourself. We certainly haven't given up on your baby. Everything that we can do is being done for her. Mary you were . . . Mary you're calling her, aren't you? . . . Mrs Heenan, try to hear what I'm telling you . . . Nurse! Nurse!'

The woman on the bed was still breathing, and showing few signs now of pain. Five minutes later the brief life of the tiny scrap called Mary had flickered and been extinguished. And the frail craft on the bed was drifting further and further out to sea, soon, before their eyes, to reach a high sea that was untroubled: without pain, without fear, without feeling.

'He's in the waiting room, is he?' Dr Sharkey asked the sister.

'Yes. His wife told me he's never wanted to be present at any of the births.'

'How much was he told?'

'I don't know. *She* was told of the danger, but when I asked what she'd told her husband she got . . . well, cagey.'

'It's a common enough reaction. It's a way of shutting their own eyes to possibilities, as well as their husband's . . . Telling him's going to be difficult.'

He looked at her. She had sometimes in the past relieved him of the responsibility.

'Oh *please*, Dr Sharkey. With both of them gone, I couldn't find words. It'll be better coming from a man.'

He pursed his lips, then nodded. He composed in his mind the ragbag of phrases he had used on other similar occasions. Then he straightened his shoulders and went into the corridor.

In the waiting room, surrounded by scruffy piles of newspapers and magazines, there were three men, sitting in postures of anxiety familiar to the doctor. Two were young, one probably still in his teens. The third was a middle-aged man slumped forward in his chair, his chin cupped in his hands. Dr Sharkey went up to him.

'Mr Heenan?'

The man looked up and then rose. He was of middle height, broad in the shoulders, with a round face formed to be seen over a pint mug, or swapping jokes with a pretty girl. But now he looked stunned, as if he had not slept for hours. The doctor had seen victims of major accidents, and their rescuers, who looked like that. Almost shell-shocked.

'Is it over?' he asked eagerly, in a thick voice that broke with emotion. 'Boy or girl? Ellen's fine, is she? She'll be wanting to see me.'

'Could you come to my office, Mr Heenan?'

'I'd rather see Ellen first.'

'This way, please.'

The doctor gave him no choice, but held his arm as he guided him along the corridor, round two corners, and into his office. The man let himself be led, walking heavily, with a slight limp. When they were both inside, Dr Sharkey propelled him into a chair, then got a bottle from a bottom drawer in his desk and poured him a small whisky.

'What is this, Doctor?' Heenan asked, eyeing the bottle. 'Is there something wrong with the babby? We've been lucky so far, God be thanked. Tell me so I can go to her.'

The doctor waited until he had had a swig of the whisky.

'I'm afraid it's worse than that. I don't know how much your wife told you . . .'

'Told me? What about?'

'Ah, I see. It's often the way.' The doctor swallowed. 'Well, your wife was told some time ago that there would be problems with the birth. And not just to the baby, but danger to herself as well.'

Heenan looked at him as he came to a halt. He echoed his wife's protest.

'*No!*'

'I'm afraid so. The birth was as difficult as we feared, and . . .'

'They're both gone! Aren't they? Tell me straight! They're both dead, aren't they?'

'Yes, Mr Heenan, I'm afraid they are.'

'Oh, God!' The man howled his outrage and keeled forward. Dr Sharkey let him sit thus, his face in his knees, his shoulders heaving. He seemed to be saying something, but all Dr Sharkey could make out was something that sounded like, 'Oh God, I have sinned.' He thought he must be making a mistake.

'You won't want to be hearing medical details as yet,' he said at last, feeling that the shuffling of his little cards of conventional phrases was leaving them increasingly threadbare. 'Take another little drink of whisky . . . it *does* help, even doctors admit that . . . Then perhaps you'd like to be driven home.'

He poured another quarter of an inch into the glass, then

came round and handed it towards the hunched, unhearing figure. As he stood over him, he distinctly caught Heenan's words: 'Lord, I am punished, justly punished.'

Sharkey took him by the shoulder, pulled him upright, and thrust the glass into his hand.

'Get that down you, man. Remember you'll need all the strength you can muster to tell your children. I'll try to find someone who can drive you, and a car.'

Five minutes later, two ambulance drivers, a man and a woman, arrived at Sharkey's office, raised Heenan tenderly to his feet, and led him out to the waiting car. Sharkey wondered whether he was in a fit state to go home, but didn't see what else he could have done. This was the winter of 1979, ancillary workers were on strike, all the hospital services at the Leeds General Infirmary were working at full stretch. He hurried back to Maternity to monitor the progress of a woman who was about to be delivered of twins.

As fast as was consonant with compassion, the ambulance people bundled Heenan towards a car.

'That's a bad limp you have,' said the man.

'Got it in a fire. Used to be a fireman,' mumbled Heenan.

It was almost the last piece of normal talk they got out of him.

The woman ambulance driver got into the back of the car with Heenan. She tried first administering comfort, then attempted to stiffen him for the ordeal ahead. Nothing she said seemed to get through. He muttered over and over again: 'I am justly punished.' The woman looked into the driving mirror and saw the driver's eyes looking back at her.

'What should we do?' she whispered.

'What can we do?' He shrugged, not unsympathetically. 'There's no spare staff at the hospital. We're needed there. We'll go in with him . . .'

At last they drew up at the address they had been given. It was a detached house in Rodley, a minute or two from the ring road. It looked as if it had been built between the wars; the paint was peeling and the plaster beginning to crumble in places. But it was a roomy house, quiet apart from the hum of traffic, and beyond it lay fields and a small wood. The ambulance woman registered that it was a better house than she had expected the man in the car to live in: a good place to bring up children in, she thought.

'Mr Heenan,' she said gently. The driver had got out, and was holding open the door.

'What? What?'

'Mr Heenan, you're home. Your children will be wanting to know what has happened.'

'Oh, my God.'

He heaved forward, put a foot out of the car and stumbled out on to the road. He looked around him wildly. The woman had briskly got out her side, and now took his other arm, and together they began leading him to his front door.

'Courage, Mr Heenan. For the sake of the children.'

'Oh God, it's not courage they need. It's their dead mother, God rest her soul.'

Before they could get to the door, it opened. They had been watched for from the window. A boy and a girl stood in the doorway.

'Dad!' said the boy.

The woman from the ambulance understood at once that they knew.

'Can you get your dad inside?' she said. 'He's very upset.'

'Oh God,' he mumbled. 'My poor children.'

The children stood aside and they manoeuvred him with difficulty through the door.

'Where can he go?' the driver asked the girl.

'In here, the sitting room. He'll need time. It's the shock.'

'Can you show me the kitchen?' the woman asked her. 'I'll make a cup of coffee.'

'He prefers tea. I'll make it. I know how he likes it.'

The woman realized with a shock that it was the children who were taking charge, the father who was being mothered. She let the boy settle his father into an armchair in the sitting room and followed the girl to the kitchen.

'You know, don't you?' she asked, as she watched her at the cupboards.

'Yes. He wouldn't be so upset if it was just the baby.'

9

'He seems to be terribly shocked.'

'Mummy told us, you see. The doctor warned her there might be problems with the birth and . . . danger for herself. But she didn't tell Daddy. She said he was worried about his job. And he lost it two months ago.'

'What did he do?'

'He was foreman on a building site. He said they didn't want to sack him, but with the re –'

'Recession?'

'Yes – they had no choice.'

'So he's still out of work?'

'Yes.'

'Well, I suppose he'll need all his time looking after you.'

'Yes. Shall we take the tea in?'

'I'll help you. What's your name, by the way?'

'Anne. They call me Annie.'

When they came into the sitting room with the tray, Annie's father was sitting with his elbows on his knees, staring ahead, muttering to himself. When his daughter put the tray down on the table beside him and began pouring, he gave her one look, and tears came into his eyes.

'Oh Annie, what have I done to you? And Matthew? To all of you?'

The eldest boy was sitting beside him, his hand on his arm. The younger ones were watching, frightened. The ambulance driver stirred in his chair, and raised his eyebrows at his partner. She looked around, uneasy, but unable to think of anything else they could do. The man got to his feet and approached the group of the man and the two older children.

'Well, Mr Heenan, I'm afraid we'll have to be going. You know how things are at the moment. We'd like to offer our sympathy to all of you – sincere sympathy.'

There was silence. The man looked at his cup. Then, the words seeming to be wrung from him, to come from some barely remembered convention of behaviour, he said: 'Thanks for all you've done.'

Later, in the car, the ambulance woman, unable to find words for her unease, said: 'I hope he gets a grip on himself.'

The man nodded, not unsympathetic, just overworked and exhausted.

'He'll bloody have to, won't he?'

'The children seemed to cope better than he did.'

'They don't understand, do they, not in the same way — about money, and getting help, and whatever . . . The whole bloody system's breaking down,' he added bitterly.

As soon as they got back to the infirmary they were called out to a woman who had been battered half to death by her husband. Even the woman let the Heenans slip from her mind.

Annie and Matthew were frightened. They had encouraged, coaxed, forced their father to drink some tea, and he had got down perhaps a quarter of the cup. Now he sat once more, hunched forward, staring ahead. From time to time he muttered things — words, phrases, something to do with 'punishment'. They didn't understand. They didn't see their mother's death as a punishment — not for her, not for any of them. It was a disaster, but unrelated to anything they had done. Scared by the silence, they sent the younger children out to play in the back garden.

'But play *quietly*,' they said, with some rudimentary understanding of the decencies of death. Then they cleared up the tea things and went out to the kitchen.

'I don't know what to do,' said Matthew.

'Nor do I.'

'We've never had anything to do with death.'

'Except Aunt Lucy's. And we didn't even go to the funeral.'

Aunt Lucy had left them all her house. She had been a jolly, loving aunt, but she had died three years before, and their memories were becoming dim.

'Dad will have to look after us now,' said Matthew.

Annie was the manager, the realist. She had been her mother's great help in keeping the younger children clean and tidy. Now she looked straight into Matthew's eyes.

'What if he can't cope?'

'He'll *have* to cope,' said the boy fiercely. They washed the cups and saucers under the tap, and put them on the draining-board to dry. 'There were those children in my class who were put into care.'

'I know. The Mortons.'

'None of the teachers could control them.'

'They were dreadful.'

They said no more. There was nothing else to do in the kitchen, but they didn't want to go back to their father. They stood by the sink, looking at each other.

'Maybe he ought to go to bed,' said Matthew.

'It's only half-past six.'

'Yes, but he's not well. He ought to go to bed and rest, so that he can think about it and . . . accept it.'

Annie voiced the fears of both of them.

'He doesn't sound as if he ever will.'

'He's got to come to terms with it,' said Matthew, talking very adult, and using a phrase he'd learnt from television.

'Perhaps we should try and persuade him.'

Reluctantly, they went back into the sitting room. Matthew leant over him.

'Dad . . . Dad? Would you like to go to bed, Dad? It's been a shock to you . . .'

'It's been a shock to all of us.'

Again the words seemed to be wrung from him.

'Not so much for us. You see we knew.'

Knew what?'

'About Mum and . . . and the danger. She didn't want to tell you, with you being so worried about your job.' His father gave something between a grunt and a sob. 'We think you ought to go to bed and get some rest.'

'It's more than rest I need . . . Forgive me, Lord.'

'Will you come up with us?'

'Aye . . . Aye, I'll go up.'

Little by little they got him up the stairs. He would stop after one or two steps and say, 'Are the young ones all right?' or, 'You've something for your suppers?' Finally they got him to the landing and steered him towards the door to the big double bedroom.

'I can't sleep there!'

The words were bellowed out.

'Dad!'

'I can't sleep there! Not where I used to sleep with your mother, God rest her soul. Annie, I'll never sleep there again.'

They looked at each other. Then they steered him to Gregory's little bedroom. Once inside, Annie retrieved the boy's toys and books which were scattered around, while Matthew persuaded his father to take off his jacket, then his trousers. They fetched his pyjamas from the big bedroom, but they found him sitting on the bed in his shirt and underpants, sobbing. They put his legs up under the blankets and sheet, and he lay down docilely, like a small child. But when Matthew turned in the doorway before switching out the light, what his father reminded him of, on the bare bed frame in the narrow room, was a picture of a monk in his cell in a religious book his mother had treasured.

He and Annie tiptoed downstairs and watched the smaller ones in the twilit patch of garden at the back.

'We've got to think what to do,' said Annie.

There was no problem about getting the smaller ones to bed. Their play had been solemn, and they seemed to welcome bed as a chance to absorb their new, motherless state – or perhaps to escape from it to sleep. The smallest one, Jamie, really did not understand. Jamie usually shared the second bedroom with Matthew, though Matthew had always intended to assert his right to a room of his own when his brother was older. Daddy being in Gregory's room presented problems, and Matthew proposed to solve them for the moment by having Jamie in with him in the big double bed that Daddy said he would never sleep in again. Jamie cried, though, and said it was too *big*: he did indeed look tiny in it, and perhaps it brought home to him some sense of his loss. In the end he was put into Matthew's room with Gregory, and Matthew faced the prospect of sleeping in the big bed on his own. Annie, the only girl, had always had a room to herself.

When they had been tucked up for the night, and talked to, Matthew and Annie crept along the landing and listened outside the smallest bedroom. They had hoped for silence, but what they heard were sobs and muffled words and phrases. White-faced, they tiptoed downstairs.

'He'll get better,' said Matthew, louder than he intended, but still sounding unsure.

'Yes, he's bound to,' agreed Annie. 'He's strong.'

They both knew they were contradicting themselves, were merely cheering themselves up.

'Of course he is,' Matthew said, his voice still too loud. 'He'll get himself together. Look at all the overtime he did, when he was afraid of losing his job.'

'That's right. It's just that sometimes he looked the weaker one, beside Mum.'

'She shielded him. Took things on herself and kept them from him.'

'There won't be anyone to do that now.'

The conversation seemed to be taking a direction unwanted by either of them, but they were powerless to turn it back.

'It may take him a while to recover,' said Annie.

'We'll have to get him to the funeral. Somehow.'

'Funerals,' said Annie. 'It's the little baby's too.'

'Dad didn't want another. Though he never said.'

'We none of us really wanted another – not even Mum.'

'It's Mum's death that's upset him . . . I suppose the dole money will just keep coming in, will it? Could we phone Social Security and ask them to send it here? Or does he have to go and collect it?'

'Surely he'll be able to go and collect it? He wouldn't want us to starve.'

'He doesn't sound as if he can think straight about anything at the moment . . .' He looked at her, the worry now undisguised. 'If only people don't start asking questions – while he's *like that*.'

'We can cope with Greg and Jamie,' said Annie.

'Of course we can. But they'll say I'm only thirteen . . . I wish I knew more about funerals.'

'Couldn't you go and talk to Father Muldoon about it? And perhaps you could bring up the dole then, or go to him after.'

'I don't think we should go to school tomorrow. I don't think you *do* till after the funeral.'

'I suppose not.'

'I'll go and talk to him . . . I suppose if he's still like this we'll have to cover up. Perhaps do it for a few days.'

'Yes.' Annie looked at him hard. 'We've got to do something. We mustn't all be taken into care.'

He gazed back, then nodded determinedly.

CHAPTER 2

The Funeral

The next morning the children got up with fear in their hearts.

Matthew made the breakfast while Annie got the two younger children dressed. Gregory had cried himself to sleep, but then had slept soundly through. Jamie still didn't understand, and kept saying 'Mummy?' Annie thought it would be best not to try and explain: perhaps eventually he would just stop saying 'Mummy' and say 'Annie' instead.

They had cereals and toast as usual. Uncertainty made them nervous, silent. Matthew made a big pot of tea, and the question of who should take tea and toast up to Dad was there in the air. With a heavy heart, Matthew decided it was man's work. When they heard the lavatory flush he put two rounds of toast on a plate, poured out a strong, sweet cup, just as his father liked it, then went slowly upstairs.

Dermot Heenan was sitting on the bed, in his underclothes, staring ahead.

'How can I eat?' he muttered. 'Why should I keep myself alive?'

'For us,' said Matthew urgently.

'By God, don't you know you'd be better off without me?' came the thick mumble.

Matthew looked at him, and a tingle of fear went up his spine. He turned and left the little bedroom.

When breakfast had been eaten and washed up he rang the presbytery at St Joseph's and spoke to Father Muldoon. He had heard the news from the hospital chaplain, and had known more about the danger to the lives of mother and unborn child than Dermot Heenan had done. He was sad for the woman and her family, and he said soothing words to Matthew that were not the less sincere for having become standard with him.

Matthew had to concentrate hard, determined to get it right.

'I wondered, Father, if I could come and have a talk with you – about the funeral, and that.'

Father Muldoon's surprise showed in his voice.

'You, Matthew?'

'Well, Dad and Annie have their hands full, you see.'

'I'm sure they do. I could come round to the house –'

Matthew had to stop himself saying, 'No' too loudly and too quickly.

'I think it would be better, Father, if I came round to see you. The little ones find it difficult getting used to the idea of Mummy not being there, and Annie and Dad are trying to take their minds off things.'

Father Muldoon was used to eldest children in large families shouldering adult burdens early in life. He accepted the position more readily than Matthew had expected.

'I see. Well, I'm free at eleven.'

At eleven prompt Matthew was ringing on the presbytery doorbell. He still had the black tie he had been bought when Aunt Lucy died, and he had on his blue school blazer and grey trousers. Father Muldoon didn't quite know what to offer him, but he put a mug of Nescafé in front of him, and the boy sipped at it as they talked quite composedly about the funeral.

'Dad's so upset he doesn't want to talk about it. I wondered if you could help with the arrangements, Father.'

He meant, 'if you could arrange it all'. Father Muldoon was used to doing that. It happened often enough, especially with lonely old people. He talked the situation over with Matthew, especially the father's unemployed state, and then arranged something simple and decent for the following Thursday.

'Your mother and father both had an insurance policy towards the cost of funerals in the family, I know that. And

17

the parish has a fund that might help a bit with the rest,' he said. 'Will there be many family members coming, do you think?'

'I don't think so,' Matthew said, glad to be able to say that truthfully; glad that there was hardly anyone to ask questions. 'Mum has – had – a brother and a sister in Ireland, but I don't think they'll come over. Dad had Aunt Lucy, but she's dead. All our grandparents are dead.'

'Perhaps we'll have two cars for family, just in case.'

'I wanted to ask about money, Father.'

'Money? Well, as I said, there's this fund –'

'No, I don't mean the funeral. I mean for food and that. Housekeeping. Now Dad's all we've got, he won't be able to work, will he? They won't force him to get another job?'

'Oh, I wouldn't think so. Not with the four of you to look after. Your dad needn't worry about that. I tell you what, there's someone in the parish – Nan O'Connor, you probably know her – works at the Social Security office. Would you like me to make an appointment for your father to go along and see her?'

'If it's not too much trouble, Father.'

So by the time he left he had an appointment for his father to talk over the situation with Mrs O'Connor on Monday at ten o'clock. Of course, it was Matthew who went.

She was surprised at first, but the boy was such a little adult, and he explained very sensibly about his father being so upset, and having to be both mother and father to the little ones, that she readily talked over the situation with him.

'What about the dole money?' Matthew asked her.

'Well, it will become National Assistance now, because your father couldn't take a job even if he could find one.'

'No, that's right. He's at home all the time now, and very upset. Annie and I do all the shopping. Could we collect the Assistance money for him?'

'Well, it's unusual . . . But you could get authorization from your father.'

'What would he write? Could you write it for him?'

'Oh, I think so. Then you could just get him to sign it.'

Matthew thought Dermot could probably still sign his name. He felt emboldened by success.

'We know the postmaster at Calverley,' he said. 'There shouldn't be any problem.'

'There are other benefits that you could well qualify for as a family,' said Mrs O'Connor as she typed the note. 'I'll look out the forms.'

'Could you fill out the forms as far as you can?' Matthew asked. 'Or I'll come in and do them with you? My dad's a builder. He's not very good at that sort of thing.'

She agreed without a qualm, and the two began a relationship, liking and understanding each other. Or thinking they understood.

By then there had been no improvement in Dermot Heenan's mental state. When they took him his food he mumbled about not wanting to live, about being worthless and damned, about their being better off without him. When they collected his tray they found he had hardly done more than toy or nibble, often not even that. Sometimes Annie sat on the bed and forced him to eat, forking it into his mouth. 'You've got to eat, *for us*, Dad,' she would say – to get the predictable reply.

Sometimes they heard him go to the lavatory. They never heard him washing.

Washing became urgent as the day of the funeral approached. The night before, when the little ones had had a shower, which was what they preferred, Matthew and Annie ran a bath. Annie fetched her father, then left it to Matthew to get his clothes off and get him into it.

'What's all this for?' mumbled his father.

'For the funeral, Dad. The funeral's tomorrow.'

'I can't go, Matthew!' he said, turning as if to run away. 'I can't see her buried! I killed her!'

'Of course you didn't kill her, Dad.'

'As good as.'

'You'll have to go, Dad. What would people think if you weren't at the funeral of your own wife?'

'Don't give a curse what they think.'

But he let himself be undressed and put in the bath. While

he was washed he kept muttering about his sinfulness, about the damned not being wanted in church. When he was washed and dried, Matthew got him into pyjamas for the first time since the deaths. When they got him into bed, and without talking about it, Matthew and Annie went and prayed together by Annie's bed, as they had not done since they were small children.

Next morning, by unspoken agreement, Matthew left making the breakfast and getting the small ones ready to Annie. He had the major task. He put his father's best suit – his only suit – over the bannisters, then fetched him a cup of tea from the kitchen. It was pointless to waste time trying to force toast down him. He was sitting on the bed, in a familiar position, bent forward, gazing ahead. When he saw Matthew with a cup in one hand, his suit over the other arm, he began whimpering.

'No, I can't go, Matthew. I can't see her buried.'

'You've got to go, Dad. I've got your white shirt here too. Stand up and we'll get you into it.'

'I tell you I can't go to church, Matthew. I can't.'

Matthew tried a new tack. He stood over him like a schoolteacher.

'Dad! Get up and get dressed!'

His mother had sometimes treated her husband like another of her children. In their hearts the children had always known he was the weaker of the two – easily led, inclined to take the easy way out. He was used to others taking decisions for him. When he heard the steel in Matthew's voice he stood up. Matthew breathed a short sigh of relief.

'Right . . . Get out of your pyjamas . . . Here's your shirt.'

When he had got his father dressed, he told him to sit in the upright chair under the window; not on any account to get back into bed. Before he closed the door, he turned and saw his father begin to slump forward again. Downstairs, Annie was washing up, having sent Gregory upstairs to dress Jamie and himself – as an experiment, to see if he could. She looked up at Matthew as he came into the kitchen and he nodded.

'He's dressed. We'll get him down nearer the time.'

'Thanks be to God,' Annie said. It was one of her mother's phrases.

'He's mentally ill. He ought to see a doctor.'

They looked at each other. It was a thought they had tried to avoid. The phrase 'into care' seemed to hover in the air between them. They put the thought from them. Annie let the water out of the sink and went upstairs to change and see that Jamie looked decent. They hadn't wanted to take him to the funeral, but they couldn't think what else to do with him. The immediate neighbours were out at work all day, and they'd never been close to Mrs Heenan.

At a quarter-past ten they both went up to their father's room and stood in the doorway.

'Dad. It's time.'

He took some seconds to register what they were saying, then he made to stand up, lurching forwards. They took an arm each and led him downstairs. When they took him into the living room little Jamie, spruced up and scared, looked at his father as if he couldn't remember who he was.

'Poor kids!' muttered Dermot Heenan, wiping his eyes with his sleeve. 'Poor bloody kids.'

At that moment the two black cars drew up outside. Matthew led his father to the front door, and then out to the car where a black-suited man was holding the door open.

'Matthew!' whispered his father urgently. 'I'll go to the service. But I can't see her put in the ground.'

Matthew thought for a moment, then let the attendant shut the door on his father. Matthew ran towards Annie and the two small ones, going towards the second car.

'He says he'll go to the service but not to the burial. It might be better. People would try to talk to him. You go home with him in the first car, and I'll go to the churchyard.'

Annie thought for a moment, and then nodded. Matthew ran back to the shiny black limousine and let himself be put into the back seat with his father. He whispered sharply: 'Stop mumbling, Dad.'

The funeral was a nightmare. Dermot Heenan stumbled from the car and up the steps of St Joseph's, his head seeming buried in his bricklayer's chest, looking neither to left nor right. In the pew at the front to which they were led, he slumped forward in his usual position, holding it with redoubled persistence since it prevented him from seeing the full-sized and the diminutive coffins standing before the altar. Matthew hoped it would be thought he was praying – as perhaps he was. The church was quite full. Ellen Heenan had kept up links with the Irish community in Leeds. Dermot's Irish links were three generations in the past, but his social life was centred around the Irish Club in the York Road, apart from occasional visits to the pub with his mates from work. Ellen had been a regular churchgoer at St Joseph's, and had taken the older children. Dermot was more occasional, but both were popular. People were sorry at Ellen's death, and sad for the motherless family, and they came to pay their last respects and to express their sympathy. Matthew and Annie rather wished fewer had come to see their father in his present state. They felt they couldn't look around, but they sensed still more people coming in after their arrival.

Father Muldoon spoke simply and well. He talked of Ellen's womanly love for her family, her modesty, her sense of duty. He said she was a model Catholic wife and mother. He expressed the congregation's sympathy for the bereaved family, and said that he himself, who was shortly to return to Ireland, would always remember Ellen Heenan as a fine example of motherhood such as that country knew so well how to produce.

Annie pulled down Jamie's little finger, which was going up his nose. From the end of the pew she heard her father groan. She thought: we're not thinking about Mummy at all. Father Muldoon is up there talking about her, but we're thinking of something else entirely. How to put a good front on. How to get by without people realizing about Daddy. And yet she was everything to us. She fed us, clothed us, loved us, wiped our knees when we fell over, wiped our eyes when we cried. And now she's gone, and we're not even thinking about her at her funeral.

But then she thought: Mummy wouldn't have wanted us to be taken into care.

The service ended with 'Eternal Father, strong to save'. When the congregation rose to sing, Matthew patted his father on the shoulder, as if to say: 'Don't try to stand – everyone knows you're too upset.' When the coffins had been taken from the church the mourners waited respectfully for the family to leave. Matthew gave his father a gentle shake, and he got up and charged out of the church, down the steps, and into the waiting car – his bolt-hole, his nest, his womb. The children followed at a more seemly pace, and Annie ushered the younger ones towards the first car. As he got in, Greg looked at his father with a sort of baffled curiosity.

Matthew stood for a moment at the top of the steps, small and frail-looking, waiting for the first car to move off and the second to come forward. He could see the hearse with the coffins already trailing up the hill in the direction of the Catholic churchyard. He felt a sudden spurt of fear at being the only one of the family by the grave.

'Your dad is obviously very cut up by your mum's death.'

Matthew looked round quickly. It was Harry Curtin, a burly man with a kindly face, who had been his father's employer. Matthew knew he was not a Catholic, so coming to Ellen Heenan's funeral was a good deed that required special effort.

'He is,' said Matthew simply. Then he thought he ought to add something. 'But he'll get over it. He can be quite strong really. Like when he did all that overtime last year because we needed extra money with the baby coming.'

'You don't do ov –' Curtin began. Then he stopped. He was conscious of Matthew throwing him a quick, puzzled glance. 'Yes, of course. I'm sure you're right. Your dad will find the strength.'

'Thank you for coming,' said Matthew, as the second car drove forward and he walked down the steps and got into it, feeling very small and alone.

The ceremony at the graveside was most terrible of all. When the car arrived at the churchyard the driver directed

Matthew to the newest part of the ground, where he had known his mother would be buried. The two coffins were already being lowered in, and Matthew dawdled over, conscious that other cars were arriving. He told Father Muldoon his father couldn't face the burial. Then he stood at the foot of the grave, trying not to look down, sensing a little knot of people gathering behind him. Father Muldoon read the brief words of committal, but it was as he scattered earth over the coffins that Matthew broke up. Now he did not have to worry about his father the terrible truth about what had happened to them suddenly overwhelmed him. Simple words hammered themselves into his head: We loved you, we've lost you. Consciousness of everything their mother had done for them, and the love she had had for them, filled him, and brought with it a knowledge of the dreadful gap she left, a gap that he and Annie would have to strive inadequately to fill for the younger ones. But there was a gap in *their* lives too, and there was no one to fill it for them.

And another feeling followed – a sort of anger. I should not be here now, alone, Matthew thought. This isn't something I should have to bear. We should be given support, not have to be giving it. And not hiding things, contriving, lying. His face crumpled, and he looked down as his father did into his chest. The weight on him seemed insupportable.

A hand on his shoulder told him it was over. He righted his face, wiped his eyes, and walked back towards the car. Father Muldoon, with a lifetime of experience, judged it was best to leave him to himself. But as the little group around the grave broke up, Matthew, about to get into the limousine again, found that someone with less understanding than Father Muldoon had caught up with him. He heard a coarse voice behind him say: 'I'm sorry your father wasn't here, because I did want to express our condolences.'

Matthew turned, to see a woman whom he felt he knew slightly – someone who occasionally came on Sundays to St Joseph's. She was dressed in a dark grey suit and had on a purple hat which did not seem quite suitable. She was smiling encouragingly, but her ample figure seemed somehow intimidating rather than comfortable, her breasts aggressive pyramids through the white blouse. Matthew was disturbed by something about her which he could not quite put his finger on but which later, in bed that night, he was to identify to himself as something sexual.

'Yes, Dad is very cut up,' he said, using Mr Curtin's phrase.

'Well, he would be, wouldn't he? I expect you all are.' She smiled again, an overdone, uninviting smile. 'Will you tell him specially that Mrs O'Keefe expressed her sympathy? Said if there was anything she could do . . .'

'Mrs O'Keefe. Yes, I'll tell him,' said Matthew, getting into the car.

But as the car drove him slowly home Matthew was not thinking about Mrs O'Keefe. He was remembering his brief words with Harry Curtin outside the church. Harry Curtin was liked by the Heenan children. He'd often dropped in on the house in Calverley Row when their father was working for him, sometimes bringing sweets, and had always been cheerful and listened to what they wanted to tell him. He'd been genuinely sorry when he had had to lay their father off. Matthew felt he knew him.

And he was sure that what he had started to say when Matthew had mentioned overtime was: 'You don't do overtime in a recession.' Or, 'You don't do overtime when you're about to be laid off.' Only he'd stopped himself just in time. Or not quite in time. Because Matthew felt quite sure that was what he'd been going to say.

CHAPTER 3

Carrying On

When Matthew and Annie came back to the house in Calverley Row for the last time, in the summer of 1993, he was a rising executive of a printing firm but uncertain about his future; considering a change of direction. Annie was a housewife, reluctantly working four mornings a week in a kitchen shop in Newcastle to help with the mortgage. They were let in by Jamie and they settled down to wait in the sitting room, getting the same sense they always got of having stepped back in time. The fat, stuffed chairs and sofa were that bit shabbier, the wallpaper was that bit more faded; the only new things were the odd ornament or photo in a frame. One of these last showed Matthew being presented to the Queen at the opening of his firm's new printing works in Northampton. But essentially it was the house in Calverley Row, just as it had been when they had become its masters in 1979.

'How are the children?' Matthew asked, as Annie poured tea.

'Oh, fine. Jeremy has had the measles, but he's over them now. They're both loving school . . . Ted's very good with them, but they'll be missing me.'

'Of course they will. Funny, isn't it? Your having a second family, with Jamie not yet grown up.'

'It's not a *second* family, Matthew — it's my first! My own. It's all I ever wanted. They try to make you feel embarrassed about saying that these days, but it's true. I'd have been a terrible career woman. I only go out to work because we need the money . . . About time you started, Matthew.'

'No,' said Matthew – not bleakly, but decisively. 'I've done all that – been a parent, looked after kids. Having another family now would be like going back.'

They were silent for a moment, remembering.

'Incredible how we just took over, isn't it?' Matthew said. 'Took it all on, just like that.'

'We didn't have much choice,' said Annie. 'At least, that's how we saw it.'

'It didn't even occur to us that people were going to start asking questions about Dad.'

'Oh, it did – quite soon. I remember we talked about it in this room. Talked about it, and made plans about what we should do. I think most things that we could reasonably expect to happen we had plans for. We did a remarkable job. What happened was' – she stopped, her face troubled – 'was something that we couldn't have foreseen.'

But that wasn't entirely true as far as Matthew was concerned. In the days following the funeral he was attacked at times by doubts and forebodings, mainly springing from those words of Harry Curtin's on the steps of St Joseph's. Of course he did not foresee precisely what was to happen; that would have been impossible, but he was very conscious that there was something in the background he did not know, things that he did not understand, and he had a vague sense that those things – whatever they were – would catch up with them at some stage.

He did not share those doubts and fears with Annie. Partly this was because he saw no advantage in two people being burdened with worries instead of one. Partly he was assuming the male role in a Catholic marriage – a role his father had never quite managed to fill.

Getting Jamie into a crèche was easy enough. The church ran one at St Joseph's primary school, which Greg attended, and they were naturally anxious to help the motherless family. Either Matthew or Annie went along with the two youngest every day before going off to their own school, which was the state one on the other side of the ring road. There was a supermarket quite close to the house, across a field and a coppice, and twice a week one or other of the older children would walk over there with a list. National Assistance money came in each week, and there was no problem getting it from the Calverley post office – only making it do. Annie had been taught elementary cooking by her mother, and she had a repertoire of basic dishes which she started to teach Matthew. There were several old cook books from the early days of the Heenans' marriage, and she went to those to start doing more difficult things: stews, roasts, even pies. They taught Greg to do easy things, so quite soon he took over the breakfast toast, and sometimes peeled potatoes or carrots. When all else failed there were hamburgers – but not too often, Annie said severely. She was very like her mother. In fact, she took her place so readily that quite soon the two figures became confused in the younger boys' minds.

The washing presented no problems either: Annie had long ago mastered the machine. Further ahead they could not look. She taught Matthew how to use it, because the more skills they shared, the more the jobs could be varied, and boredom kept at bay. House cleaning came low down on the list of priorities, because they did not plan to let anybody in to the house if they could help it. Annie decided on a blitz every first Saturday in the month. Keeping everybody clean and well turned out was much more important. That was what people *saw*.

In the weeks after their mother died, one or other of them went to church on Sundays, while the other looked after the smaller ones. Father Muldoon asked benevolently how things were going on at home, and they always answered brightly and mendaciously. But six weeks after their mother's funeral, Father Muldoon was to take up his transfer to an Irish parish. This became the subject of a late-night discussion between Annie and Matthew.

'There'll be a new priest coming,' said Annie. 'Someone who doesn't know about us, or about Mum and her death.'

Matthew thought this over.

'Father Muldoon might mention us to him.'

'He might. Or leave some kind of note. But even if he

does, it could be ages before the new priest asks about us. Perhaps he'll just assume we've moved away.'

'If we stopped going to church, you mean?'

'Yes . . . I don't want to. But if we don't go people won't be reminded of us every week. They might wonder for a bit, but eventually they'll probably assume we've moved away.'

'They'll see us around – in the supermarket, and that.'

'Some will, now and again. I just mean that the less people see us, the less they're reminded of us; the less danger there is of anyone starting to ask questions.' She added, as if she were serving up the wisdom of ages: 'Out of sight, out of mind.'

Matthew thought. Annie, sitting there putting the practical case, made him feel inadequate – the improviser rather than the planner. But she was quite right. Everything had to be thought through now.

'I think you're right,' he said at last. 'And I think it would be best not to go to Father Muldoon's last service next Sunday. There'll be lots and lots of people there, so he won't notice if we're not. If he actually saw us, or one of us –'

'It might jog his mind to mention us. That's right. I don't think we should go to church any more.'

So Father Muldoon left St Joseph's unfarewelled by the Heenan family. He had been a popular priest, the church was full, and everyone there was anxious to take a personal leave of the man. He certainly didn't notice the absence of the Heenans. But he was a conscientious man, and as a matter of routine he did leave a note about them with his occasional secretary for his successor. The successor was from the south, a young man bent on promotion, with very different ideas about pastoral care from his Irish equivalents. He read the note, but since he never saw the Heenans, he never followed it up.

The neighbours presented a different problem to Matthew and Annie. Not the immediate neighbours, for the Heenans had never been on more than nodding terms with them, and they were out at work all day. But in the little street of fifteen or so houses they had been on chatty terms with two families: the Claydons at number eight and the Purdoms at

29

number four. Mrs Claydon had been their mother's friend – not close, but the neighbour she would choose to gossip with of a morning; swap recipes with, tell the various ailments of her children to. She had been at the funeral. It would be natural for her to take an interest in Ellen Heenan's children.

Mr Purdom was their father's friend. Not a drinking crony or anything like that: in so far as he had friends of that sort they were his workmates on the building site. But Mr Purdom had known their Aunt Lucy; took an interest when they moved into the house on her death, and was generally a comfortable, undemanding sort of chap that Dermot could borrow gardening tools from, give racing tips to, or swap condemnations of the government with. He was one of those who might ask questions when he never saw Dermot Heenan. That was what they had to guard against.

There was no question of their father being seen, that was for sure: there would be no more visits to church, and even a walk along the road seemed out of the question. He was more of a <u>shambolic</u> mess than ever – a muttering, weeping, shaking figure whom they sometimes forgot to keep clean and shaven because they had so much else to do. Matthew tried now and then to sit with him and talk. He'd try it for five minutes, but when he got no more than thick self-accusations, sobs, cries that he would be better off dead, he would give up, and confine his attentions to the difficult business of getting food down him. There was no set pattern to his father's instability. Sometimes he would say a sentence that surprised them by its clarity, or disturbed them because they only partially understood it. 'I never liked it, you see, when she was pregnant,' he said once, with disconcerting bluntness, 'never liked doing it with her.' But it led to nothing, seemed to come from nothing except his self-lacerating meditations. In general, he sank further and further into a world of his own which meant that he could not be produced for the benefit of the real world of Calverley Row. Matthew and Annie knew in the back of their minds that he needed help – help of a kind they could not give him. But they never spoke of that.

So when they discussed the matter, they agreed that the

30

best thing to do was to keep him in people's thoughts by reminding them of him – and how arduous his responsibilities now were. And that was what they did. Annie would go along to Mrs Claydon's with a sugar bowl in her hand.

'Dad says could you lend us a little bit of sugar till he gets to the shops? We're right out, and the children do like sugar on their cornflakes.'

Mrs Claydon went to get some, smiling a little at 'the children'.

'Don't bother to return it. How are Greg and Jamie getting along? Are they beginning to accept it?'

'Yes, they do. Dad's got Jamie into the nursery school, so he can take any little jobs that might come up. Jamie loves it there, and it makes us all freer.'

'Tell your dad if there's anything I can do . . .'

Matthew, coming home from school, passed Mr Purdom giving the front lawn the first mow of spring.

'Dad did ours yesterday,' he said chattily. 'He said he's never done it so early.'

'I know. I couldn't believe that it needed doing. How is your dad? Is he coping all right?'

'Oh, yes. He's got Annie and me to help him. I think he misses being out at work, but perhaps he'll be able to take a job when Jamie's bigger.'

'Tell your dad if there's anything we can do . . .'

So, in the neighbourhood, they gave a shadowy, bravely-coping existence to a father who was becoming more and more of a human wreck in the little bedroom upstairs. For the two eldest, it had the elements of a game: they had to restrain themselves from going to borrow things too often. It could give the impression that the family was becoming disorganized.

'Just mention Dad casually,' said Matthew. 'In passing.'

That's all they needed to do at school, where their father was barely known. 'How's your dad coping?' their form mistress would ask sympathetically. 'Oh, fine,' they would say. 'He's learning all the time,' Annie would sometimes add. There was no danger of Jamie saying anything to arouse suspicion, but Greg had to be coached. 'Dad does everything for us now,' they told him to say. To one kind teacher at his school he blurted out, 'Annie's our mum now,' before adding the standard piece about Dad. He was too young for the teacher to examine the two statements and wonder whether they were a mite contradictory.

People occasionally rang, because the people at St Joseph's made up a caring little community. Luckily they never compared notes and realized that it was never Dermot who answered the phone.

One day when Annie answered it, there was a hard, common-voiced woman on the line.

'Oh – hello. That's – is it Mary Heenan?'

'I'm Annie.'

'Oh, well I'm just ringing to see that you're all all right.'

'Oh yes, we're fine.'

'Getting over the awful loss, are you?'

'Oh yes, we are.'

'Could I speak to your dad, do you think?'

'Dad's out. He's very busy.'

'Of course he is. Well, tell him Mrs O'Keefe rang. And if there's anything I can do . . .'

'We'll let you know,' promised Annie, putting down the phone.

The woman's voice, which she said to herself was a *pretend* voice, made her vaguely uneasy. She didn't mention the call to Matthew, on the principle they both followed of not mentioning vague feelings of unease, only concrete things they could do something about.

And so, for the children, life went on if not as usual, then with a good semblance of normality. Only Annie and Matthew felt that burden of responsibility, that sense of contriving, hiding and lying which seemed to signify the end of their childhood, and sometimes made Annie long to be able to go to church. 'It shouldn't be like this, should it?' she said to Matthew one evening, late in the day, and tired by physical work and the nagging load of care. 'It's not the way things are meant to be.' And Matthew said: 'No. But it's the way things have got to be . . . if we're to stop people finding out about Dad.'

Always in their minds, then and later, there was the question of how long things could go on like that.

Even in 1993, when they sat in their old sitting room, listening to Jamie coping in the bedroom above them, and running up and down the stairs with athletic grace, they speculated about how things might have gone on.

'I wonder how long we could have got away with it,' Matthew said, 'if *she* hadn't started poking her nose in.'

CHAPTER 4

That Woman

'Why, it's Matthew, isn't it? Matthew Heenan? I've been thinking so much about you all.'

Matthew turned and saw the woman from the cemetery.

He and Annie had talked things over, and they had agreed that they had to have, just now and again, some time to themselves: time to do normal things that children of their age did – visit friends, kick a football, mooch around the shops. So on alternate weeks, one or other of them would be free after school on one day to do whatever took his or her fancy. It would be better all round for them to be seen, from time to time, doing normal things, not giving the impression that they were tied to the house. So at half-past three Matthew had taken the bus along to Horsforth and was strolling along the main street, buying the odd tube of Smarties, gazing into a sports shop window and thinking about the approach of summer.

'Yes,' he said, turning round reluctantly, but trying to hide it with a display of openness. 'That's right.'

'I was at your mother's funeral, remember?'

'Yes. At the cemetery.'

'And at the service – though you wouldn't remember, there were so many there. Your mother was very well thought of – much loved.' The words were said flatly, as a mere formula, as if she couldn't be bothered to make any effort to appear sincere to a mere child. 'I was sorry not to be able to tell your father that at the cemetery.'

'He was very upset, you see.'

'So you said. And we could all see that. I'm sure everybody

34

understood. Death takes different people different ways. I lost my own mother recently, so I know. I hope your father's coming to terms with it now.'

She spoke in the tones and phrases of the newspaper advice column, as if this was the closest she could come to imagining the emotions of grief and loss. But Matthew did not notice that. What he noticed – because his eyes were on a level with them, and had started noticing such things generally – were her breasts, which were full and round, like hard melons under the thin pink blouse. When he looked down, confused, he saw her legs – shapely, stockinged, attractive. He found himself blushing, hastily looked up again, and caught a half-smile on her full red lips. It was a smile that suggested they were sharing a shameful secret.

'Oh yes, he's coming to terms with it. He's got all of us to look after, you see.'

'Of course. It must be a tremendous b – . . . a tremendous responsibility. He'll never have a moment to himself.'

'Not really. There's so much he has to learn how to do.' He should have stopped there, but during his repetitions of this sort of line he had become conscious of how overwhelmingly boring and overworked he made his father's life sound. There was a danger of the Catholic ladies banding together in some sort of scheme to take some of the work off his shoulders. So he added: 'When Annie and I are a little bit older he'll be able to leave us and go out for a pint sometimes in the evenings.'

The woman nodded, still with the half-smile on her face that he had seen when he'd been caught looking at her legs.

'That's right,' she said. 'In fact I'm sure you're quite old enough to babysit now.'

'Dad says not,' said Matthew hastily.

'Oh, I think he's being silly. Over-cautious. The eldest one in a big family is always good with the smaller ones. You get a sense of responsibility, don't you?'

'I don't know about that . . .'

'I'm sure your dad would be all the better for a night out.' She smiled, her teeth flashing brilliantly through the two gashes of red. 'I'm going to come round to yours and drag him out one of these days . . .'

'Oh, I don't think he'd go –'

'We'll see about that.' She smiled, but it wasn't a joking kind of smile. 'A man's got to get out now and again. Maybe we should wait until my Rob's home. But I'll come round and see how you are – see if there's anything I can do.'

'Well –'

'Ta-ta. Must rush. I've got to pick up a dress that's being altered for me, and it's nearly five.'

And with a wave she clattered off down the street, her bottom wiggling under her tight skirt.

That evening, when they were alone, in the precious time when they could unburden themselves, Matthew told Annie about the woman. By then he had had time to meditate the effect she had had on him. He ended: 'She says she's coming round, to see if she can help.'

Annie said with a confidence she didn't entirely feel: 'We'll tell her everything's under control.'

'It's not easy to tell her. She's very pushy.'

'Who *is* she, anyway?'

'I'm not sure. She mentioned a husband called Rob. Did Dad used to go drinking sometimes with someone called Rob O'Keefe?'

'I remember the name.'

'I think this must be his wife.'

'I don't remember Mum having anything to do with her. What's she like?'

'Horrible!' He tried to get his thoughts in order. 'Like she comes too close, puts herself all near you, and –'

'You mean like –?'

'Sexy. Like she always does that to any man she is with, so she does it even with a schoolboy.'

Annie thought.

'Perhaps that's a good thing. I mean, if she's that sort why should she concern herself with how we're getting on; whether we're fed and clothed properly?'

Matthew could think of a reason, but he kept it to himself.

It was as a logical consequence of that reason that Matthew

decided that he needed to talk to Harry Curtin again. His father's former employer was operating with a much-slimmed-down workforce, but he was still in business. He had a son at the same school as Matthew, and on the pretext that his father might be looking for a job before very long, he found out that Curtin was working on the construction of a small block of offices off Town Street, Stanningley. Telling Annie he had something important to do which he'd tell her about if it came to anything, Matthew managed to be around there about knocking-off time. He kept a watch from the doorway of a shop, and when Harry Curtin came out some minutes after his workmen, Matthew ran and caught him up.

'Hello, Mr Curtin.'

Harry Curtin swung round and stopped.

'Hello, Matthew. Didn't expect to see you in this neck of the woods. What brings you here?'

'Oh, I've been to see Mrs O'Connor at the Social Security office. I do a lot of that sort of stuff for Dad – he doesn't understand about how to claim, and that.'

'Yes, he's better with his hands, is your dad.'

'That's right . . .' Matthew had decided not to prevaricate, and he plunged straight in. 'He's explained about the overtime, Mr Curtin.'

Harry Curtin shuffled, embarrassed.

'Oh, did you understand . . . ? I didn't mean . . .'

'Well, I saw that you were surprised, and that he hadn't really been doing overtime, like he'd told us.'

Harry Curtin took a deep breath, still embarrassed, but seeming relieved.

'Well, I didn't want to upturn the apple cart, not at your mum's funeral. So long as you've got it sorted out.'

'He was making Christmas presents for us. The wooden train for Greg, and the doll's house for Jamie. In a friend's garage, so we wouldn't know. He didn't want to spend a lot of money last Christmas because he had a suspicion that he might be made redundant before very long.'

'Well, that explains it, then, doesn't it?' said Harry Curtin heartily. Too heartily, Matthew wondered? 'Might have known it would be something like that. How are you all getting on now?'

'Oh, fine. Dad's learning all sorts of new things.'

'I bet he is. It's good to know he's coping.'

'Oh yes. He did wonder if there might be a part-time job in the future.'

'Well, we'll have to see. When the general election's out of the way things might pick up. It'd mean his hands were full.'

'Oh, he'd have to get a bit of help in the house, but Jamie's at day nursery now, and people are very good.'

'It's nice that they're rallying round. I suppose it's people from your church, is it?'

'That's right. They just drop in now and then to see that things are going on all right. I saw Mrs O'Keefe the other day.' From the corner of his eye, Matthew saw Harry Curtin shoot him a look. 'She said she'd be dropping by.'

'Well, that's nice. That's very good,' stumbled Harry. He was conscious that he wasn't very good with words when he was uncertain or embarrassed, and he was fearful that he had given something away to the boy for the second time. Matthew relieved him of his embarrassment.

'Oh, excuse me – I think that's Jason MacIntyre.' And he darted off down a side street after the figure of a boy whom he didn't know from Adam.

Matthew debated with himself whether to talk the matter over with Annie. He would have liked to have kept it from her, but really he didn't have much choice. He had told his sister that there was something he was looking into, and it would be impossible not to tell her what it was. When she was on to something, Annie could be very persistent. And from another point of view, it was something of a relief to share his suspicions. Matthew felt all too often these days that there was a great and multifarious burden on his shoulders, and one they were too slight to bear for long. So he told her that night when they were alone.

'It was Mr Curtin at the funeral set me thinking,' he said.

'At the funeral? You never told me.'

'Well, that was because I was just thinking, wondering.

When I mentioned Dad doing all that overtime last year, he seemed surprised, and then he covered it up.'

Annie frowned, not understanding.

'Surprised? But that's what Dad said he was doing.'

'Yes – *said* he was doing. Well, today I took Mr Curtin up on it. I said that we'd found out that what Dad was really doing was making Christmas presents for us. And Mr Curtin seemed relieved it was all explained – or maybe relieved it was explained in that way, and we believed it. But then I just mentioned Mrs O'Keefe and he – well, he looked at me quickly.'

Annie thought. She saw quite soon the direction his thoughts were going.

'It's not much.'

'Then he got all sort of hesitant and stumbly and embarrassed. That's when I took off.'

'You mean it was like he *knew* something . . . about Dad and Mrs O'Keefe?'

'Yes. Or suspected.'

'That they might have been . . . having an affair?'

'Yes.'

There was a silence between them.

'The *bitch*!'

It was a word that their mother had occasionally used under provocation. Annie's bitterness summed up feelings that had been growing in Matthew since the talk with Curtin.

'Yes,' he said. 'And what about *him*?' He raised his eyes to the ceiling. 'Going with someone else while Mum was pregnant and sick and afraid she was going to die.'

'I'll never trust him again.'

'There's nothing left to trust . . . But we've got to be careful about *her*.'

'Why?'

'Because she might be more persistent than other people. And if it suited her purpose she wouldn't think twice about telling people about us if she knew what was going on here.'

'So if she comes round we mustn't show how we feel about her, you mean?'

'No. And we mustn't let her find out anything at all.'

'That won't be easy, not if she keeps coming round. How can we stop her if she does?'

'I don't know . . . We'll have to think about that.'

She came a week later. The doorbell rang about half-past five and there she stood, in a tight blue skirt just down to her knees and a revealing yellow blouse of the sort their mother used to say that married women didn't wear. Her face was caked with pink make-up and her lipstick was shiny, disturbing. In fact, Matthew felt not only disturbed but intimidated.

'Dad's not here –' he began, but she pushed past them (they made it their habit, when possible, both to go to the door when they were uncertain who it was, but it had been to no avail in this instance), and now stood in the kitchen as if inspecting the preparations Annie was making for tea – sausages and mash.

'My, I can see you're a fine little cook! Your dad must be awfully proud of you.'

'Dad's not here –'

'Well, I'll just wait for him in the front room.'

And she marched down the hall and into the drawing room, where Greg and Jamie were zooming round the floor playing with the (commercially manufactured) train Greg had got at Christmas. They looked at her with unabashed curiosity.

'Oh, little dears,' she said, and sat down in one of the two armchairs. Matthew and Annie sat down too, on the sofa opposite her. Annie was seeing her closely for the first time. She's not dressed for a visit to a family that's lost its mother, she thought. She's dressed to attract – to attract men. She looks tarty. That's what Mum used to call women who dress like that and she was right. She's disgusting.

'Dad's down at the Social Security office,' said Matthew, feeling he would have to find new places for him to go.

'At this time of day?'

'He's got a special arrangement with Mrs O'Connor.'

'*Has* he?'

'And then he's going on to Harry Curtin's, to talk about a part-time job.'

'Doesn't seem to mind leaving you on your own. You said he thought you were too young to babysit.'

'Oh, at night,' said Matthew. 'This is daytime. That's different, isn't it?'

'Maybe,' said the woman, with a puzzled expression on her face. 'So when are you expecting him home?'

'We're not really. He said it was a case of "expect me when you see me."'

As he said this, Matthew felt the sharp stab of reality: that was something his father had said very often during the months of their mother's pregnancy. And he'd said it because he and this woman . . . The remembrance knocked another nail into the coffin of Matthew's respect for his father.

'Well, like I say, it's obvious you can cope,' said Mrs O'Keefe, looking round the room and forcing a look of concern on to her hard face. 'Looks clean and tidy to me. Mind you, I'm not one who believes in wearing themselves out dusting and scrubbing. My Rob always says: "It wasn't for your skill as a charlady I married you, Carmen." Isn't he awful? He's on the rigs at the moment, so I get a bit of peace.'

She looked around the room again, seeming to have run out of things to say, but still reluctant to go.

'I suppose if you don't know when he'll be back . . .'

'No, we don't.'

She thought, her face becoming calculating in the most obvious way. 'I tell you what: it's obvious he feels he can leave you on your own, so there's no reason why him and me shouldn't have an early evening drink. I think I'll set a day –'

'Oh, I don't know –'

'Say next Wednesday. I'll be here next Wednesday at six, in the car, and we'll go for a quick drink at the Lamb.'

'I don't think we ought –'

The woman suddenly went still. The children were so used

41

to occasional regular noises from upstairs that they had ceased to react to them. It took a second or so for them to realize that Mrs O'Keefe was reacting to the sound of the flush from the upstairs lavatory. When they did, they stiffened too. She looked around the room, where all four children were, and then directly at Matthew.

'So who the hell's upstairs then?' she demanded.

CHAPTER 5

The Threat

'Oh, that's just Auntie Maureen,' said Matthew.

He asked himself when the woman had gone where the lie had come from. He asked himself the same thing fourteen years later when he was back in the house for the last time. He could not account for it other than as some kind of inspiration, or gift of God. True, he had been naggingly conscious for some time that the lies he was telling were becoming horribly repetitive. And certainly both he and Annie realized how easy it would be to be caught out in a lie, and perhaps had prepared subconsciously a second line of fantasy as a defence. Yet it still seemed to him that Auntie Maureen was born in an instant; the creation of Mrs O'Keefe's question, the generous gift of a beneficent power, giving them temporary breathing space. Matthew never lost his belief in that power, watching over them, protecting them, in spite of all that happened later.

'Who the hell's she?' Mrs O'Keefe demanded belligerently.

'Oh, she's just come over to help look after us for a week or two,' said Matthew.

There was a moment or two's silence, tense and strained, as the woman digested this. Only Matthew and Annie were conscious that Greg was looking at them too, an expression of puzzlement on his small face.

'I thought you said you were alone in the house?'

They took up the challenge together.

'We are — as good as,' said Matthew.

'She gets horribly seasick,' said Annie. 'She's useless for days afterwards.'

'We're looking after her more than she's looking after us,' chimed in Matthew. 'Always up and down to the toilet. I expect when she gets over it she'll be more use.'

'Pity she doesn't fly,' said Mrs O'Keefe.

'Oh, she's terrified of flying.'

'Then she should bleeding well stay put, shouldn't she?'

It occurred to Matthew that the woman believed in Auntie Maureen, but resented her. No doubt it was the idea of another woman in the home of her – But he shut his mind to what his father was, or had been, to this horrible creature.

'Oh, she's not the type to do that,' he said airily. 'She's desperate to help. Even when she's not very much.'

'Oh well, I suppose your dad knows what he's doing, inviting her here,' said Mrs O'Keefe, clutching her handbag and getting up to go. 'She's not a permanency, is she?'

'Oh, no. She's got her own house, near Dublin. But her children are all grown up.'

'Sounds like the motherly type,' said Mrs O'Keefe with a sniff. 'I never went in for motherly instinct myself . . . though I want to do my best for you lot, of course.'

The children stayed silent.

'Well' – Mrs O'Keefe was palpably reluctant, pausing at the sitting room door – 'I suppose I'd better be going . . . if you really don't know when your dad will be home –'

'We don't.'

'Now, mind you tell him. I'll be round to fetch him next Wednesday at six, for a nice quiet drink in the Lamb. No need to hurry ourselves, is there, if you've got dear Auntie Maureen to look after you. Your dad must be desperate for a pint and a bit of adult conversation.' They were in the kitchen again by now, and she was throwing these vaguely insulting scraps at them as they ushered her towards the back door. 'Mind you tell him. Wednesday at six. And tell your Auntie Maureen I shall look forward to getting to know her.'

When the back door was shut and – after a suitable interval – locked, Matthew leaned his head against the cold, distempered wall of the kitchen, conscious that his shirt was dripping with sweat around the armpits. He felt he had just gone

44

through a long and vicious fight; one all the worse for not being a physical one. This woman was an opponent, and a dangerous one. When he straightened himself up, his eyes were still damp from the emotions of strain and frustration. He said to Annie: 'We've got to think what to do.'

Again. They both realized they were now much deeper into the undergrowth, with the advent of Mrs O'Keefe and the invention of Auntie Maureen. Mrs O'Keefe – *that woman*, as they henceforward called her among themselves – was clearly someone who would push herself into the house, would ask questions about everything, and was already smelling rats. Auntie Maureen, having been mentioned to her, might need to be substantiated by further fantasies, either for Mrs O'Keefe, or for others. And further fantasies meant further possibilities of being caught out.

They slept on it, and first talked about it next day, in the five minutes they could walk together between dropping Greg and Jamie off at the primary school with the nursery and the school gate where they separated to join their different groups of friends.

'I think we've got to refuse to let her in,' said Annie, taking up the subject without preamble the moment they could.

'So do I. We can't let her in over and over again and find new excuses as to why Dad isn't at home. Quite apart from "Auntie Maureen".'

'"Auntie Maureen" we can drop. We only said she'd be here for a week or two.'

'I suppose so. She's dangerous. There's probably people at church who know we haven't got an Auntie Maureen.'

'We could say she's not a real auntie, just called that. A friend of mother's perhaps. But I agree, she's dangerous. It was brilliant, you inventing her, but we'll have to drop her.'

'That doesn't help about *that woman*. We've got to find some way of stopping her visiting.'

'The trouble is, I can't think of a reason.'

'Can't you?'

'I mean, Dad . . . went with her while Mum was pregnant. You'd think he'd be pleased to see her again.'

'Would you? Then why do you think he's like he is?'

They stopped walking, and Annie looked at him.

'Well, with Mum dying, and the baby . . . I mean, it sent him off his head . . .'

'With guilt. For having . . . done that with her while Mum was pregnant. He said once when I was there that he hadn't enjoyed . . . *it* while she was pregnant. I bet it was then that *that woman* went all out to get him, and now he's gone mad with guilt.'

They started walking again.

'I think you're right. But what do we do?'

'We *never* open the door again. Keep it locked, and the chain up. Tell Greg he's never to open it. When she comes we'll just shout through it.'

'But what shall we say?'

'That Dad has forbidden us to let her in.'

Annie thought again, then turned to him, smiling. 'I like the idea of that.'

In the days that followed the plan was sophisticated somewhat. Both front and back doors were left permanently locked, and they shouted, 'Who is it?' before they opened it. There were few enough callers. If it had not been for the threat of Mrs O'Keefe, the children might have felt that interest in them and their affairs had all but died away. The milkman, coming for his money on Thursday evening, expressed his approval.

'You're careful who you open the door to, are you?'

'Yes, we are.'

'That's very sensible. Dad not in?'

'Not at the moment. He generally goes to see Father Coffey on Thursday evenings.'

The milkman was not a Catholic, so he was unlikely to learn anything that contradicted this last statement. None of the family, in fact, had ever seen the new priest at St Joseph's, and they tried to avoid members of the congregation. Annie had perceived the milkman as a danger, since he was the only person who called regularly at the house. She was pleased when he nodded unsuspiciously, took his money and walked away. She regarded her remark as another of those inspirations, though the fact was that both she and Matthew were getting better at lying.

They had no doubt that *that woman* would arrive on cue, and the older ones were very tensed-up on Wednesday evening. At five-to six a car drew up in the road outside, and Matthew and Annie went to the kitchen. They positioned themselves close to the door, and listened as the front gate clicked and high-heeled shoes came clip-clop down the path.

The knock on the door was loud, authoritative. They left a second or two before they called out:

'Who is it?'

'It's Carmen O'Keefe, Matthew. Come to take your father out for a treat.'

That last touch enraged him. His voice came louder than he had intended.

'He isn't coming. He says that we're never to let you into the house again.'

There was a moment's silence outside.

'There's been some silly mistake, Matthew.'

'No, there hasn't,' shouted Annie. 'He says he never wants to see or talk to you again.'

'Is your father there?'

'Yes, he is.'

'Let me in. I want to talk to him.'

'No. He's told us we mustn't. He says he'll never have anything more to do with you.'

'Go away! You're horrible!' This contribution came from Greg, attracted to the kitchen by the shouting. Annie felt he detracted from the seriousness of the occasion, and bundled him back into the front room.

Again there was a moment's silence.

'Look, there's some mistake here . . .'

'No, there isn't.'

'Your dad's misunderstood something I've said.'

'No, he hasn't. He says you're disgusting. He says he'll never have anything more to do with you as long as he lives. So go away and don't come back.'

A pause of indecision, then the heels, emphatic with indignation, clip-clopped back down the path and out through the front gate. The children stood looking at each other as they heard the car start up, turn in the drive, then charge out of the cul-de-sac which was Calverley Row.

'We've won!' said Annie.

'For the moment,' said Matthew.

But it did seem for a time as if they had scored a magnificent victory. Nothing more was heard of Carmen O'Keefe. They expected her to call or ring, but she did not. The only time the telephone rang, it was their mother's brother in Ireland, and his interest was purely perfunctory: when he heard they were all right he said he would tell his sister and rang off with assurances that they could always call him if there was anything they needed. He had never had anything in common with Dermot Heenan, and didn't want especially to speak to him.

So Mrs O'Keefe seemed to have gone out of their life as decisively as she had come into it. They thought about it and talked about it and came to the conclusion she must have realized from their words that their father was disgusted with himself over what he had done while his wife was so close to death, and quite naturally did not want to have anything more to do with her. Any danger that she might guess at the real consequences that the affair had had, they put to the back of their minds.

But they kept up their precautions. The door was always locked, and even if they were in the garden they locked the door from the outside, for fear that she might arrive and simply march in and go upstairs.

'It was like a prison,' said Matthew, all those years later, as he marched up and down the front room, the young, apparently confident manager of a business that was somehow managing to hold its head up during another terrible recession. 'For a time after she'd come into our lives and then gone out, it was like being in prison. We'd locked Dad away, but we'd locked ourselves away with him. I suppose that's what prisons are: they lock up the keepers with the criminals.'

'What I wonder at, today, is how well we did,' said Annie, calmly knitting away at some children's clothes she had

48

characteristically brought with her. 'After all, we knew far less than twelve- or thirteen-year-olds know today. There's far more sex on television nowadays – it's sort of taken for granted, even in the hours when young children are watching. And of course, Mum had kept us rather protected. Yet somehow we managed to hit on the right note to keep her away from us.'

'What – you mean, "He says you're disgusting"?'

'Yes, that kind of thing.'

'It must have been something intuitive – though of course we didn't know the half. But it was the right note to strike. And it certainly kept her quiet for a time. Long enough for us to start coming out of our prison.'

'If she'd been wise, she would just have kept quiet and kept away. If she had, everything would have blown over. Or at least we wouldn't have been involved.'

'But she wasn't wise. Wisdom wasn't in her,' said the wise-beyond-his-years Matthew.

Annie nodded. She had a schoolteacher husband and two children of five and three. The events of 1979 were now an episode of past history, one she could talk about almost as if she had not been involved. For Matthew it was the shaping experience of his life.

'She brought us face to face with evil,' he said.

CHAPTER 6

Asking Questions

All this time, as the evenings began to lighten and the spring flowers blossomed and faded, the man in the smallest bedroom remained in much the same state of mental darkness. It became easier to get him to take food, as if he was resigned to continuing his own existence, and he sometimes had what could be called good days as well as bad ones: then he might say something like, 'I should be doing something for you kids,' or, 'God knows how you're coping without your mother.' But these moments of realization that the situation in the house was exceptional, was out of kilter, were rare indeed, and mostly he lay or sat on the bed mumbling about punishment and sin. It was as much as they could do to prevent him becoming smelly, like a neglected dog.

As the weeks dragged by, and the feeling of being imprisoned grew, Matthew's attitude to his father changed: when he first suspected that he had been having an affair with the sensual, threatening creature who was now disturbing their security he had felt a childish rage and disgust. How *could* he betray their mother like that? The inevitable daily contacts with the shambling mess matured and modified that reaction: he still felt contempt, but now it became tinged with compassion. The wrong he had done had brought on him a dreadful punishment. He said one day: 'You shouldn't blame yourself.' It was something his mother had sometimes said; for example when a boisterous children's game in a tree had led to a younger friend falling and breaking his leg. But Dermot had merely mumbled something that sounded like, 'Who else?' Matthew had shrugged and left the frowsty little room.

Of friends there were now only those at school – children to talk and play with during set hours. Once they might have come home with the Heenan children after school, or called at weekends. Ellen Heenan had loved having troops of children around her. Matthew and Annie made sure that didn't happen now: 'Dad's got too much to do,' they said, 'we don't want to add to his burden.' Or sometimes: 'We haven't got over Mum's death yet. It's no fun in our house now.' Even children could realize they wouldn't be welcome.

'I don't think she's going to come back,' said Matthew to Annie one day in the kitchen, washing up tea things.

'Nor do I. But I wish I *knew*.'

'We can't ask her to give us a signed oath that she won't come round and bother us again,' Matthew pointed out.

'I don't mean that. I mean, I wish I knew what she was doing and saying. About us.'

Matthew nodded vigorously.

'So do I. If she's saying anything. Maybe she thinks the sensible thing is to keep quiet.'

'Maybe. But she's not a sensible person. I wish I knew . . . In fact, I wish we knew a whole lot more about her. We hardly know anything.'

'That's a point. Not that I want to. But maybe we *need* to know about her. As a sort of weapon.'

'That's right. Because if she knew about . . . about *here*, she'd dob us in to the authorities just out of spite. Not because she cared, but to get her own back.'

The next day, later in the evening, as they talked together like any married couple with children in the hours after bed-time, Matthew said: 'If we could go to church together, talk to some of the people we know there . . .'

'We agreed we wouldn't.'

'If we could go together – it would give the impression that everything was all right at home.'

'I suppose so. But what about the new priest?'

51

'We could slip out the side door. A lot of people do if they're in a hurry to get away. He won't know everybody yet. There's no reason why he should wonder who we are if we're careful.'

'No . . . It's not what we decided . . . But I would like to go to church. It's what Mum would have wanted.'

'I know. I keep thinking how we're forgetting her.'

'Yes. Jamie has forgotten her entirely.'

They looked at each other, a little tearful.

'I think we should go to church. Just the once.'

'And try to find out about that woman afterwards.'

'But who would look after the little ones?'

'Greg will have to look after Jamie.'

It wasn't what either of them wanted, but they could not think of an alternative. They made it a very serious business – it was a first time, and a sign of their trust in him. They were both going to have to go to church – Greg accepted going to church as a normal part of life – and he would be totally responsible for his brother. They were both to stay in the living room with a selection of toys, but as a precaution, all kitchen implements or utensils that could be shut away were, because they were sure that at some point one or other would want something from the fridge and go out there. Any little cuts or bruises, Greg could deal with – sweets and Elastoplasts were left on the table – but if anything serious happened he was to run along to Mr Purdom or Mrs Claydon. But he was to try not to. As they left, they waited to make sure Greg locked the back door, as he had been told to.

It was funny to be back at church again. It was a ten-minute walk, and as they arrived there people were drawing up in cars or arriving on foot. Somehow it was both strange and yet normal to be part of that throng again – strange because their mother was not with them, and people obviously felt a certain awkwardness with them; normal because the throng of people was there with a common purpose which they recognized and shared. 'Hello, Annie; hello, Matthew – everything all right?' people said, looking at them closely and registering that they were neat and tidy, as they had taken good care to be.

'Yes, everything's fine. People have been very good. Dad's at home looking after the littlies,' they said.

'Never a great one for church, your dad,' someone said.

'Not really, though Mum tried.'

'People have been good, have they?' Mrs O'Hara said. 'I've felt awfully guilty myself −'

'Oh, they've helped a lot,' Matthew said hastily.

'Because someone was saying only the other day they hadn't seen your dad since the day of the funeral.'

'Oh? Who was that?'

'I think it was Mrs O'Keefe. But she's hardly ever here herself − not what I'd call a regular. Hardly a Catholic at all. I think she must have meant she never saw him at the shops or supermarket.'

'They must just have missed one another,' said Annie.

They slipped into St Joseph's and registered the people in the congregation whom they knew best. Mrs Wainwright was a good talker and a casual friend of their mother's, and she was there towards the back of the church without her husband. They slipped into the pew beside her. She turned and registered the neat, conservatively-dressed pair: Matthew serious, Annie smiling up ingratiatingly. Annie was a sturdy girl, without any great pretensions to prettiness, but she could present herself attractively. She had gone to great pains to do just that. She had an end in view, and when she had that she could show great flair and determination.

'Matthew! Annie! This is a nice surprise.'

'We thought we ought to come. It's been a long time.'

'Yes, it has. And your poor mother would have wanted you to come. Dad's at home with the young ones, is he?'

'That's right . . . Is that the new priest?'

'Yes. I don't know him at all well yet, but he seems to be very good.'

She said it as if evaluating the performance of a new quiz show host. Matthew and Annie looked at each other as the service began. There would be no need to use the side door after the service. They could just tag along with Mrs Wainwright, if the priest didn't know her well: he would assume they were with her, were her children. The two began murmuring a prayer.

The service, even with a new priest leading it, seemed familiar and comforting. It was a still point in a shifting, uncertain, uncomfortable world. To say and sing well-known words seemed like something to grip on to. When the service was over they trooped out in Mrs Wainwright's wake, and outside in the sunlight they shook hands with the priest.

'Hello, Mrs –'

'Wainwright.'

'And –?'

'Matthew and Annie.'

'Hello, Matthew and Annie.'

That was all. It was dead simple. Outside, on the steps leading to the road, they looked around for people to talk to. But Mrs Wainwright stepped in with a better solution.

'Why don't you come back with me and have a cup of tea and some cake?' she asked. 'My husband's away on business, and I'm quite lonely in that big house.'

'Oh, I don't know –' Annie began.

'You go,' said Matthew. It seemed an ideal opportunity. 'I'd better be getting back to Dad. The littlies get a bit much for him after a while.'

So Matthew started off in the direction of home. People clustered around St Joseph's greeted him in a friendly way, and one of them said: 'Tell your dad we miss him at the Irish Club.' That made Matthew think, as he speeded up to get home and assure himself that all was all right with the youngest ones. The Irish Club would be the ideal place to pick up any gossip that was going around about Mrs O'Keefe and her activities. On the other hand, he could hardly go along there on his own. Though they did from time to time have children's parties . . .

Annie, meanwhile, had started off with Mrs Wainwright. The substantial semis in the vicinity of St Joseph's were much in demand by Catholics, some of whom went to service at their church every morning. In the two minutes' walk home Mrs Wainwright picked up a neighbour, Emily Porter, a voluble spinster who lived with her aged father and kept house for him. Mrs Wainwright said that since her husband was away on a business trip, she was relieved of the burden of the traditional Sunday roast. 'It's nice, of course – but nice to give it a miss as well.' Together they all settled down in the kitchen for tea and cakes and biscuits.

'I was glad to hear that your dad's coping all right,' said Mrs Wainwright, filling a kettle and fetching down tins of this and that. 'He looked so poorly at the funeral.'

'He was very upset,' said Annie. 'And he's never liked funerals. But he's coping fine.'

'Mrs O'Keefe says no one's set eyes on him,' said Emily Porter.

'Well, they wouldn't, would they? He's Mum and Dad to us now,' said Annie, thinking of the mumbling wreck in the little bedroom upstairs – more a child than a parent. 'Mrs O'Keefe did come round one day, but Dad was out.'

'Well, you want to watch that one,' said Miss Porter with gloomy relish, wagging a finger. 'She's probably out to get her claws into your dad.'

Annie was conscious of an access of tension in Mrs Wainwright's back as she stood at her kitchen unit slicing up dark, fruity cake. That in itself told her something: Mrs Wainwright knew about her father and Mrs O'Keefe, or at least had heard rumours, while Miss Porter had not.

'Oh, she'd never manage to do that,' Annie said. 'Dad's not got over Mum's death yet.'

'Still, you want to watch out,' repeated Emily Porter, oblivious to her hostess's disapproval. 'She's shameless, is Carmen O'Keefe. Remember a couple of years ago, Mary, when it was Joe Foster she was after? Well, she was more than after. They hardly made any secret of it. People saw them all over the place, practically bolted together. Everyone thought it disgusting. And him a good Catholic, and a married man with kiddies.'

'Mrs O'Keefe has a husband, doesn't she?' Annie asked.

'Oh, yes – Rob. He's on the oil rigs. It's when he's away for long periods that she gets up to her tricks. Or mostly, anyway, because he's a bit of a fool. It's been going on for years – there's a long line of men that have known more about her than they ought to, and we only know of the Catholic ones. I think it's disgusting she still comes to church.'

'She doesn't very often,' said Mrs Wainwright, turning round to set out plates on the kitchen table. 'She wasn't there today, though her mother-in-law was.'

'Oh, is Connie O'Keefe over?' asked Emily Porter. 'That must mean Rob is back from the rigs. She'd never come over just to see Carmen. They put up a front, but they don't get on. Maybe she'll keep her in order while she's here.'

'And maybe she won't,' said Mrs Wainwright, tight-lipped.

'Yes, you're right. Easier said than done. That big strapping husband can't do it, not when he's around, so I don't suppose Connie can make much impression.'

'I don't know what we're talking about Carmen O'Keefe for,' said Mrs Wainwright, bringing the teapot to the table.

'Oh, it was just her asking everybody if they'd seen Annie's dad,' said Emily Porter, still oblivious to the tension. 'Seemed odd to me – like she was interested in him. You keep your dad on the straight and narrow, Annie, love.'

Then they dropped the subject, and Annie was glad. She felt she had learnt quite enough, and was beginning to feel awkward. She had never quite come to terms with the fact that she had a father who had affairs. It seemed all wrong to Annie, an upsetting of the proper order of things.

Back home, putting together a cold Sunday lunch ('Summer's coming – salads are nice in summer'), she said to Matthew: 'She's telling everyone she hasn't seen Dad. And asking around to see if anyone else has.'

Matthew thought, face screwed up. 'Are they taking it seriously?'

'I don't think so. Not yet. They just think he's busy – as he would be if –'

'If he was taking care of us like he should be . . . But it shows she's suspicious herself.'

'Yes. But we pretty well knew that.'

'What else?'

'She's had a long line of . . . boyfriends. Everyone seems to know a bit of scandal about her. Miss Porter didn't know anything about her and Dad, but Mrs Wainwright did, I'm sure.'

'She'll be on the "wives and mothers" circuit. It's them who'd be particularly concerned.'

'Yes. Mrs O'Keefe's husband is away most of the time. He's on the oil rigs.'

'Do you mean she's pretty open about it?'

'Yes, I think so.'

Matthew thought. 'So there's no chance of . . . using any information like that to make her keep quiet?'

'No. They say she's blatant. They said her mother-in-law is here at the moment, so she might be a bit more careful what she does. That should give us a breathing space.'

'But that's all it is, isn't it? We've got to be realistic. At some stage she's going to get *really* suspicious that no one's seen Dad.'

'Unless she loses interest. Someone like that might . . . She might just go on to another man.'

But it was an unsatisfactory situation, and both of them felt it. It was like living on borrowed time, hoping against hope. There was now, indubitably, someone who suspected that something odd was going on in the house in Calverley Row. She couldn't know – she must realize that it was perfectly possible that Dermot Heenan now hated the very thought of his affair with her, and had forbidden the children to let her in, as they said – but she had smelt a rat. And Matthew, for one, suspected that she was not the type to leave well alone.

So they went on with their unnatural life with fear in their hearts. Their deception had now become routine, like the housework and the cooking and the supervision of Jamie and Greg. Things outside the set routine were apt to be forgotten, as Matthew realized one Sunday when he went to fetch the younger ones from the back garden, and stood there surveying it, recognizing that it was on the way to becoming a wilderness.

'We can't let it go like we have done,' he said to Annie. 'People will start talking.'

That was the great danger. Their fear was the middle-class fear of fifty years ago: that people would talk about them.

'I'll do all the house duties today,' said Annie. 'You do what needs to be done in the garden.'

It was deciding what needed to be done that was difficult. The lawn was the easy thing: it needed cutting. It probably needed other things done to it as well, but getting it cut was the obvious first step. Matthew got the old hand-mower out of the shed and gave it a rough going over. There had been rain a couple of days before, so the going was hard, but it was a job he'd done quite often before and he made some kind of a fist of it. Then he raked up the clippings and took them to the rubbish heap at the bottom of the garden.

But what to do next? He knew the rose bushes should have been pruned long since, but he couldn't find the scissor-things that you should do it with. He got a carving knife from the kitchen and hacked away with it for a bit, but when he had done over one bush he surveyed his efforts and decided he was doing more harm than good. He got the kitchen scissors and cut off the dead flowers from the daffodils and tulips. Then he got the small garden fork and – after much doubt and indecision – got down on his knees and started weeding. Some weeds he recognized, some he gave the benefit of the doubt, and some flowers fell victim to his efforts. The important thing, he decided, standing up and surveying his efforts, was that the garden should show some evidence of work having been done on it. In fact, his efforts were noticed.

'Hello – er – Matthew, is it?' came from the next-door garden.

'Hello, Mr – er –'

'Lovely day, isn't it? Just right for that sort of work.'

'Yes, lovely.'

The exchange was characteristic of their relations with the neighbours they hardly knew. Matthew was glad they were not close but glad too that he had been observed going about the ordinary business of living. The light was fading, and he decided to call it a day. As he washed his hands at the kitchen sink, he noticed he had left the knife on the window ledge outside. But Annie called him from the dining room to see a really clever drawing of Greg's, and he forgot all about it. When Annie drew the kitchen curtains, as they drew all the curtains in the house every day, it was dark outside and she did not see it.

CHAPTER 7

A Discovery

'Annie!' Matthew called urgently up the stairs about nine o'clock that evening. Annie came out to the landing from the bedroom Jamie shared with Greg: he had cried out in his sleep while she was putting Greg to bed, and she had taken him in her arms to soothe him.

'What's the matter?' she whispered down the stairs.

'Did you hear anything?'

'No. Jamie woke up, and I was talking to him a bit to get him back off. What kind of thing?'

'I was in the front room, but I thought I heard something from the back. Like voices – or a voice. A sort of shout. Then like something falling.'

There was silence upstairs, then Annie came down to him, her face screwed up with consternation.

'Are you sure?'

'No. I suppose it could have been from next door. But we don't hear much from there.'

'Who'd be round the back at this time of night?'

'It could be *her*, spying on us.'

'Why spy on us so late?'

'Because the lights are on. She could have been peeping through gaps in the curtains.'

'I don't leave gaps in the curtains. You know that. Anyway she wouldn't have seen anything . . . But why would she shout?'

'I don't know. I think we should go and look.'

Their eyes locked, fearfully; then they went to the kitchen.

Matthew went to the back door and shouted: 'Who's there . . . Is there anybody there? . . . What do you want?'

There was no sound that they could distinguish. There was still the hum of traffic from the Leeds to Shipley road, and from the ring road.

'It can't have been anything,' said Annie. 'Why don't we just forget it?'

'No. It'd be worse not knowing if there's anything there. I'll go out and you guard the house.'

'No. I'll come.'

They looked at each other again, then Matthew unlocked the kitchen door which let on to the path round to the back of the house. He peered out.

'There's nothing there.'

'You said round the back.'

'Yes.'

His legs felt like lead as he stepped through the door and on to the path. As he started round to the back garden Annie came behind him and took his hand in hers. He stopped and pressed it. As they came to the corner of the kitchen wall they peered into the murk, and then – 'Christ!' Matthew's gaze had fixed on the little patch of light under the kitchen window. 'It's her!'

He had recognized the tight yellow blouse she'd been wearing when she had pushed her way into the house. He ran down to her, his heart beating intolerably. She was lying scrunched up, her face lolling down on to the stonedashed path and – cymbals clashing in his ears – he tried to turn her over. Her breast and side were disfigured by a monstrous red gash, still oozing blood. Matthew cried out, then tried to suppress his cry and stood up, leaning his forehead against the wall, his stomach retching. He sobbed and sobbed, keeping it as quiet as possible by instinct. Then he ran into the house, followed by Annie. As she locked the back door she heard him running upstairs and knew he was going to the lavatory. She stood, wondering, fearful in the kitchen, then went through to the living room, as far as possible from that terrible object.

When Matthew came down she saw that he had washed his face, but he still looked white and drained.

'We've got to think what to do,' he said.

'What can we do? We'll have to call the police.'

He looked at her, perfectly still. It was a while before he spoke.

'You realize that will be the end? There'll be no alternative then. They'll have to take us into care.'

Annie bowed her head and started to weep.

'Why is this happening to us?' she sobbed.

Matthew felt a new access of bitterness.

'Because Dad failed us all . . . I don't think we should go to the police.'

'But how can we not? The body out there . . .'

'She's dead now. She's no threat to us any longer. And nobody's going to connect her with us. She'd had a whole string of boyfriends. If her husband found out . . .'

Annie looked up sharply.

'Matthew! Do you think that's what happened? She came to spy on us, and her husband had found out about her and Dad, and followed her and –'

'*Someone* did, didn't they? It could have been him, or it could have been one of her boyfriends.'

'Who had a knife with him?'

Matthew shuffled.

'Not necessarily. I left the kitchen knife on the windowsill this afternoon. I think . . . I think it's under the body . . . I think I saw the handle.'

'Oh, Matthew!'

'As soon as she's found here, the police will find out about Dad. You do realize that, don't you? They'll want to talk to him and they won't take no for an answer.'

'I know.'

'I can drive the car.'

'Don't be silly, Matthew. Of course you can't.'

'Yes, I can. Dad taught me to back it into the drive and then to put it back in the garage.'

'I know, but that's not driving. You couldn't drive it on a real road.'

'I could.'

'Anyway, it hasn't been driven for months.'

'Yes it has, you know it has. I put it in the drive a fortnight ago to make it look as if Dad had driven it somewhere.'

'You said it was difficult to start.'

'But it started. It'll start again. There's petrol in it, plenty of it.'

'But Matthew, on a *road*. With other cars . . .'

'We'd wait. Wait until there's hardly anything on the road. Midnight or later.'

'Wait here? With . . . *that* out the back?'

'Why not? She's not going anywhere.'

It was a remark totally uncharacteristic of Matthew. Brutal humour had never been his line. It would have distressed their mother. They both of them seemed to realize the change in them, because they looked at each other and simultaneously burst into tears, Matthew bending forward and crying into his lap.

'What's happening to us?' asked Annie again, through her tears.

Matthew straightened up.

'We've got to keep control. Of ourselves. Of what happens to us. If we can get rid of her she's gone from our lives.'

'Where would we put her? Would we just leave her? Or should we try to hide her? Bury her?'

She said it with an expression of concentrated thought on her face. Matthew recognized her words as a watershed. Suddenly it was on. It was decided. They would not call the police. They would somehow try to get rid of her. Annie looked up at him and understood the change in her position. She wasn't quite sure how it had happened, but now she agreed with Matthew that that was what they must do. They had no alternative.

'Bury her, I think,' Matthew said. 'There's that big ploughed field on the way to Greengates.'

'But . . .' Annie sat for a moment, picturing the place. 'We'd have to park the car by the road and get . . . *it* out and over the wall, even before we started burying it. There's cars going past on that road all the time. Even if we managed it, the headlights would pick us out while we buried her.'

'That's true,' agreed Matthew. Then he pondered for a bit. 'What about the little wood by the supermarket? It wouldn't be so easy digging there, but I could do it.'

'Isn't it too close?'

'I don't think so. After all, everyone's coming to the super-market the whole time. They wouldn't necessarily connect it to the houses close by . . . If they ever find her . . . Do people walk their dogs there much?'

'No, because it's just beside the field with sheep. If we buried her there we wouldn't need to use the car. We could drag her across the field – on the path that we use to go to the supermarket.'

Matthew shook his head vigorously.

'No, we couldn't. She's big. She's heavy. I wouldn't have the strength left to dig.'

'But if we drove we'd have to go on the ring road. It's so dangerous.'

'I can do it,' said Matthew obstinately.

'People would see us, and see you're too young to be driving.'

'They wouldn't care, not late at night. They just want to get home. It's only the police we'd have to worry about.'

Annie recognized his determination, and accepted defeat.

'What about tools? What would you need?'

'A spade and a big fork I should think . . . I'm going to get the car out now.'

'Why, Matthew? Why now?'

'It may take a while to start. People are watching telly now. If I had trouble starting it after midnight they might get out of bed to see who it was.'

That seemed to Annie to make sense. She nodded, and sat rigid in her chair – but what was there to fear, now? She heard him fetch the car keys from the kitchen, go out the front door, and run to the garage on the far side of the house, where the road ended and gave way to field – that field across which they often walked to the supermarket. She heard him open the front gate, open the garage door, then get into the car. Four, five times she heard him try to start it. Then she heard him pause for a while. Dad had always said that was what you should do. (That was when he *was* Dad.) When he tried again, the car started, and she heard him backing it towards the front gates. He left it running. She hoped he would come back in – she hated being there on her own – but she heard him going round to the back. He must be getting the spade and fork. How could he bear to go past *that*? She heard him come back, put the tools in the car, then turn off the ignition and shut the doors slowly. Now she had the awesome feeling of a die having been cast. It was as if a door had shut decisively, or perhaps as if the ceiling had started coming down, was lower by a foot, and getting lower and lower until it eventually would crush them. Now they were committed – for better or worse, and she was quite unsure which it would be.

'I put the tools in the back,' said Matthew, when he'd come back in, locking the front door behind him. 'We'll put her in the boot.'

'But, Matthew – all that blood!'

'I know. I think we'd better put a plastic bag over her – at least over the top part. One of those black garbage bags.'

'Oh God!' whimpered Annie. Then a thought struck her. 'Matthew – what if she's still alive?'

'She isn't. She was dead when we saw her. Otherwise she'd have been breathing, choking. I went close. There was no breathing. She was dead.'

'Don't you go stiff when you die? If she goes stiff we might not be able to get her into the boot.'

Matthew's mouth dropped open.

'Oh God! I hadn't thought of that! How long is it before you go stiff?'

'I don't know.'

'I'll have to do it now. That would probably be best anyway, while people are occupied.'

'I'll help.'

He was anxious to shield her all he could.

'No . . . Well, not yet. I'll get *it* ready. Then you may have to help me round with it. I don't think I could do it on my own, and I might make a lot of noise.' He saw her reluctance.

'I'm sorry. There's no other way. You can take the legs.'

'All right . . . It'll be quicker and quieter. Don't put any lights on outside.'

It was the most horrible thing he had ever done in his life, and it was only the darkness that saved it from being simply intolerable. He averted his eyes as he fetched an empty black plastic bag from the garbage bins, but there was no avoiding seeing it when he came back to the dim light under the kitchen window and had to pull the bag over her head, down over her shoulders, past the aggressive breasts with the dreadful gashes, down to her waist and beyond. The woman was in a slumped, almost crouching position, and Matthew decided this would make it easier to get her into the boot of the car. He suddenly remembered an old door – the door from the kitchen into the hall, which his father had replaced in a burst of DIY a year or so before. It was still down the bottom of the garden, waiting to be taken to the dump. He ran into the gloom and with difficulty brought it back to the house. He laid it on the ground by the body, then – with manifest physical reluctance, for he hated touching her – he pushed and shoved the body on to it, using just his feet when he could. He surveyed his work with satisfaction: this would make it easier for Annie to help him to get it into the car.

'Have you got a big bath towel?' he asked, when he went back into the house. 'Or a sheet? So we can put it over her and no one will know what it is if they look out of their windows.'

Annie nodded, and went to fetch a large dark blue bath towel. Matthew led the way outside, and threw the towel over her legs before Annie had a chance to see.

'Right. I've put her on that old door. You don't need to touch her. You take the bottom and I'll take the top. We'll take her to the car now and get it done with.' But as they carried the bier and the body round the side of the house he said: 'Stop. I was a fool to leave the car in the drive. We should do this in the garage. Wait here a sec.'

Annie didn't like to say that she had hated waiting for him alone in the house, but she hated the thought of waiting in the dark driveway still more. She heard him go round to the front; heard the sound of the car being driven into the garage. Then he was back. Without a word they picked up their burden, took it through the front garden and into the garage. Matthew had already opened the boot. He now pulled the doors almost to, rested the old door on the bottom of the car boot, then eased the body gently in. When he was sure there were no bits of her poking out, he closed the boot, set the door against the far wall of the garage, and then they both crept back into the house.

'So far so good,' said Matthew, as if this was some kind of boy scouts' initiative test.

'I think the waiting will be worst of all,' said Annie.

'There's a lot to think about,' said Matthew. 'How shall I dress? How can I make myself look older? Just in case a police car passes.'

That was an awful thought. They turned down the sound of the television set and sat there working it all out. Matthew fetched a cap of his father's, and found that it almost fitted, and shielded his face if it was worn at an angle. All his father's coats and jackets looked quite ridiculous on him, but he knew that his body was a boy's not a man's and had to be hidden. They finally decided on his duffel coat, which was bulky and not at all childish in style.

'I could be digging now,' he said, when they had looked at the clock for the hundredth time. 'I could take the tools over there, find a place and start digging a hole.'

'No. The tools are in the back of the car. You've been in and out of the garage two or three times already tonight. Go too often and someone's going to be looking out. Think about driving the car.'

So Matthew sat there, thinking about all his father had told him in those days when he was a real father to him: how to release the clutch slowly, gently; how to change gear without that horrible shrieking and shuddering; how to brake and secure the car with the handbrake. He'd watched his father so intently when they went out on family outings. Driving had been the symbol of his father's adulthood; of his headship of the family. Matthew had known – thought – that one day he would be head of his own family, would drive a car on family expeditions. That's how he had thought of himself, all those times he had sat in the car in the drive, changing gear, putting on the handbrake, going backwards and forwards, in and out of the garage.

They switched the television off when they usually did, and then decided to sit in the dark. But this became too spooky, because they couldn't resist wondering to themselves who else had been out there in the back garden – who it was who had done it. They crept into the kitchen and put the light on.

'That knife is still out there!' said Matthew suddenly. 'We've got to get rid of it.'

'Tomorrow's Monday. The garbagemen come.'

'That's an idea. Have we got any kitchen rubbish? I'll put it at the bottom of a bin bag and put things on top.'

They got together all the rubbish they could find, and a couple of old newspapers. Then they turned the lights off again and Matthew crept out, wrapped the knife in the newspapers, and put it at the bottom of the bag, piling the rubbish on top of it. Then he ran back to the kitchen, and they sat around the table, wondering what else they had forgotten.

Time had never passed so slowly. Impossible to do anything else, but intolerable to keep talking about the horror of what they had found and the horror of what they were about to do. From time to time they quietly opened the front door and listened to the sound of the traffic as it slowly died away to almost nothing. At ten to twelve Matthew said: 'We could do it now.'

Annie hesitated for a moment, then nodded. Matthew took the car keys, they turned off the kitchen light, then they crept out of the back door and locked it. There were no lights from the house next door or the house opposite, but that didn't mean there was no one looking out of their windows. They scuttled round to the front and into the garage. The inside of the car seemed like a refuge, until Annie remembered what was in the boot, and drew in her breath sharply.

'Don't think about that,' said Matthew, understanding at once. 'I can't, if I'm going to drive.'

The car started at the second attempt, and Matthew left it in neutral and pressed the accelerator a couple of times as he had been shown long ago. Then he pressed hard on the clutch, put the gears into reverse and swung round in the driving seat. He found he could barely see over the back of the seat, but he would not risk asking Annie to get out and guide him. He only had to go straight until he was through the gates. He prayed, then gently, slowly, he let the clutch out and backed the car down the drive, past the gateposts and out into the road.

'Marvellous!' said Annie. 'Don't forget to put the lights on.'

He had forgotten the headlights!

'Of course not,' he said. He fiddled with the little stick on the steering wheel, and eventually got some dim light. 'That should be enough.'

Darkness was what he preferred. If he could, he would have driven in total darkness. That would prevent any passing policeman seeing who was driving and stopping them – except that he *would* stop them, because it was illegal. Now he trod on the clutch again and put the car into first. Then he eased her with agonizing slowness along Calverley Row until he got to the junction with the Shipley Road. When he braked her there the engine stopped.

'Don't worry,' said Annie. 'It's still cold.'

It started at once. There was no traffic at all on the road, and Matthew's spirits rose again. But when he tried to drive out and turn right towards the roundabout, the car began that awful kangaroo motion he had dreaded. He slammed in the clutch, and then started again, releasing it gently as he turned into the still empty road. This time the car started smoothly, and they began coasting downhill towards the roundabout.

'Don't go into it unless it's quite clear,' said Annie.

Two cars sped around the roundabout on their way towards Horsforth. Matthew stopped to let them go, then eased the car into the circle, driving round the edge and then out to the right on to the ring road. Annie rather thought he should have gone into the centre of it, but she said nothing. What did it matter, with nothing on the road? They started along the ring road towards the next roundabout, where they would have to turn right again.

'I've never been in second gear,' said Matthew, his voice breaking.

'Stay in first. People will just think there's something wrong with the car.'

'No. They'll look at us. We don't want them looking.'

His heart throbbed as he put the car into neutral, then across, then up into second, as his father had often shown him, but never allowed him to do. Miraculously it worked and went smoothly in. It seemed almost as if the car was relaxing, from the tension of first gear to the mature calm of second.

'Great!' said Matthew. 'Maybe I can stay in second all the time now.'

They approached the second roundabout. There were two cars coming towards them on the ring road, but they were a long way away. Matthew drove into the roundabout, this time driving into the centre, then round it and out to the right. He didn't need to slow down much, and the car coasted along in second.

'We've done it!' said Annie. 'Nearly.'

The Greatbuys supermarket had been built on farming land a quarter of a mile from the ring road, part of the 'seventies drift out of the city centres. If this had been day time, Matthew would have needed to turn across the stream of traffic to drive into the car park, but there was no stream of traffic. He slowed down, tugged at the wheel, but as he began to turn, the car died on him again.

'Damn!' He turned the ignition angrily.

'You're still in second,' said Annie.

Matthew closed his eyes, suddenly conscious that his forehead was damp with sweat. He concentrated hard, changed down into first, then slowly eased up the clutch and drove into the empty supermarket car park. It was dark and uninviting. He turned in the direction of the little coppice of trees and the field that led across to Calverley Row and home. He parked it neatly, nose into the wall, then he braked and turned the ignition off. They sat for a moment getting their breath.

'You were wonderful,' said Annie. 'I never thought you could do it.'

But they both knew the really bad bit was still to come. Just how bad it was to be, they realized when, silently, they got out of the car, took the spade and fork out of the back, jumped on to the low wall of the car park and over into the coppice. It was pitch black in there. None of the light from the road reached through the dark trunks of the trees.

'Matthew, what if –?' Annie began.

'What?'

She had been going to say 'What if *he* is still around?' but she managed to stop herself. 'What if we dig on the edge of the field?' she said. 'Where it's not so dark.'

Matthew made a few experimental stabs with the fork, and found the going very difficult.

'I think you're right,' he said, trying not to sound relieved. 'There's nothing but tree roots here.'

When they had got through the trees and on to the edge of the field there was just a little light from the streetlights. This was pasture for sheep, and when Matthew dug the fork into the ground it was much, much easier. Not long before, it had been cultivated land. He took off his duffel coat and began loosening up the ground.

'Keep the grassy bits separate,' suggested Annie. 'So we can put them on top again.'

When he had loosened up a few feet, Matthew took the spade and began digging. Annie fetched the fork and began work on a further patch. The woman, *she*, was all huddled up, and by now she would surely be stiff. They would have to bury her like that – best, anyway, not to put her in a hole the shape of a grave. They decided that something about three feet square would be fine. Matthew dug and dug, till his arms were hanging loose from exhaustion. Annie took the spade from him and did her bit. After ten minutes he took it from her and did a second stint.

'I think that should be enough,' he said finally, standing back. 'Don't you?'

It wasn't very deep. Annie did wonder if it was deep enough. But she knew he was near the end of his strength.

'Oh yes, I think so,' she said.

They stood silent in the darkness, to summon nerve for the next stage. Across the field was home. Their street was in total darkness, but in the BP garage just down the road from them, someone had left a light on in the back office. It seemed like a sort of lighthouse, a symbol of home and safety. Suddenly Annie saw two tiny lights glinting in the coppice. She jumped, with a little squeal. Something scuttled off into the trees.

'A fox,' said Matthew. 'It won't harm us.'

Annie whimpered again.

'Come on,' said Matthew, with a false briskness. 'When we've got her in the worst will be over.'

But before that, the worst had to be gone through. They crept warily through the coppice, the blackness making their every move uncertain. The last thing they could afford at this point was a sprained ankle or arm. They jumped carefully down from the wall and walked to the car, reluctance in every step. Without a word, Matthew put the key in the boot and opened it. The body lay there, a dark mass, like some threatening, misshapen creature from a horror film, barely related to humanity but threatening it. Matthew peered into the dark recesses of the boot.

'See if we can get her out on the towel,' he said. 'There's an end here and another there.'

They pulled experimentally. The towel which had covered her lower limbs was now mostly under her, but not entirely. They pulled her towards them, but it was clear they weren't going to be able to get her out without touching her. Annie's face was twisted into a grimace.

'Try to get her up,' said Matthew. 'Keep your eyes closed.'

By tugging at the two ends of the towel, they found they could raise her up a bit, but in the end, shuddering, Matthew had to insert his arm under the body, heave it up to the edge of the boot, and then topple it over on to the car park tarmac. He had to steel himself by telling himself that it was an *it*, not a *her*: it was something he had to get rid of. The towel was still in the boot, and they laid it out beside her, then, using their feet only, they pushed the heavy, plastic-covered mass on to it.

'If only we still had the door,' said Matthew. 'But it wouldn't have gone into the car.'

'I don't think it would have gone through the trees anyway,' said Annie. 'Come on – get it up on the wall.'

They each took two corners of the towel and then, straining, lifted her up and edged her on to the wall.

'I hate that,' said Annie. 'Her being so close.'

They jumped up again on to the wall and took up their burden. The little wood seemed more impenetrable than ever, loaded with *this*. Matthew had to walk backwards, and kept tripping over roots and bumping into tree trunks. Once he started to sob with tiredness and discouragement, but Annie said, 'Come on – we're nearly there,' and he continued on until at last they came out on to the field, a few yards from where they had dug the grave.

'Can we rest?' asked Annie.

'No – just a bit longer. Come on – if we put it down we'll only have to lift it up again. Just a bit further . . . further still . . . And into the grave!'

They had reached the hole and, without ceremony, they held the towel over it, then let go two of the ends. The body fell into its resting place with a thud.

'Are you sure it's deep enough?' asked Matthew.

'Yes. Let's have a minute or two's rest, then we'll fill it in . . . Do you think we should say something?'

Matthew thought. 'What is there to say?'

'Like "Rest in peace" or something?'

He realized that she was looking on him, being male, as the nearest thing to a priest. He composed himself, somewhat self-consciously, in an attitude of prayer.

'Oh Lord, grant this woman peace,' he said. 'Come on, let's fill it in.'

The filling in was wonderfully easy, and the sense of relief was palpable as the loose earth began to cover her. They had set the grassy top clumps aside, and finally they knelt down and fitted them roughly together.

'There's a sort of hump,' said Matthew. 'But I suppose there would be.'

They stood surveying their handiwork, then they both got on top of the hump and tried to tread it down. After a minute or two, Annie said: 'Look – light.'

It was hardly that: the faintest of glimmers in the east, but it decided them. They took up the spade and fork and the big bath towel and blundered through the trees to the car.

'I feel so tired,' said Matthew, putting the key in the ignition. 'My arms ache so much they hurt.'

'You'll make it,' said Annie. 'There's nothing on the roads.'

Matthew's legs ached too, from the spadework, and the first start he made was another of those kangaroo ones that were so demoralizing. The second just about passed muster though, and they went in first gear to the entrance to the car park then straight out into the road. Concentrating hard, conscious now of something more like pain than exhaustion that had invaded his whole body, Matthew changed up into second, cruised around the roundabout and along the ring road towards home. As they approached the second round-about they became aware of a car speeding up behind them, but as they turned into the Shipley Road it sped on. Only Annie registered that it had been a police car.

When Matthew turned into Calverley Row the car died on him. He put it down into first, started it again, then kept going steadily until he turned into the drive and nosed it gently into the garage. They sat there in the darkness, too drained to speak.

'It's quiet in the house,' said Annie at last. 'Jamie hasn't woken.'

Slowly, they got out of the car and shut the doors as quietly as possible. Matthew felt a sudden spurt of something like love for the car: it had served them well, come up trumps after months of neglect. They shut the garage doors and crept round to the back door and into the house. When they switched on the kitchen light they both blinked at the strangeness of being able to see properly. It was wonderfully welcome.

'I should have a bath,' said Matthew. 'But I'm too tired.'

'You might wake the kids,' said Annie. 'You'd never be able to explain having a bath in the middle of the night. Have one in the morning.'

'One day we'll have to tell them about . . . this. When they're grown-up.'

'No, we won't. Why should we? Why burden them?'

Matthew thought, and then nodded. He took off his duffel coat and cap and hung them in the hall. Then they switched off the kitchen light and crept upstairs. Matthew's limbs felt like iron bars hanging from him, and he could hardly pull his pyjamas on. When he lay down in the big double bed, he felt at once more exhausted than he had ever been in his life yet quite unable to sleep. But within five minutes he was in the deepest of slumbers.

As the light strengthened and the sun prepared to announce its arrival, his sleep was invaded by a dream. Carmen O'Keefe was standing over him, her big, firm breasts pointing at him threateningly through the pink blouse, her red lips stretched in a smile that was no smile. She seemed about to begin an inquisition when suddenly the picture changed, and there was nothing but breasts and yellow blouse, and now they were disfigured by a bloody gash that seemed to swell and fade, enlarge and contract, then almost to shriek at him.

He screamed out, woke for a moment, then sank back into the sleep of exhaustion.

CHAPTER 8

The Irish Club

And after that – nothing. A total blank. Nobody was talking about Carmen O'Keefe. Nobody was investigating her disappearance.

That, at any rate, was how it seemed to Matthew and Annie. The day after the burying of the body, Matthew could not be woken. Annie got the breakfast and took the younger ones to school. She told Matthew's form master that Jamie had had a disturbed night and Matthew and his father had been up with him. The excuse was accepted without demur. All the teachers knew of the difficult situation in the Heenan family, or thought they did.

Matthew woke at midday, sore of limb and frowsty. He had a shower and put on clean clothes, then he went off to school to have the school dinner that they all got free. Very little entered into his head during the afternoon classes, because he was more or less asleep, but that had been quite frequently the case since his mother's death. On the way home he dropped into a newsagent's and bought the *Yorkshire Evening Post*.

There was nothing about Carmen O'Keefe. Nothing on the front page. Nothing – he ascertained this when he could sit down and go through it at home – anywhere in the paper. An event which had been the crisis, the watershed, of their lives didn't rate a mention in the Leeds daily newspaper. How could so noticeable a person disappear without arousing comment?

'Perhaps they print it too early,' Matthew said to Annie. 'We'll watch the local news on television.'

So they watched the news from Yorkshire Television. Nothing, though they sat through the whole bulletin and magazine.

'What are you watching this for?' Greg demanded to know. 'You never do usually. It's boring.'

'We've got to do an essay for English,' lied Matthew. 'On an item of local news.'

'What's an essay?' asked Greg, easily distracted on to a side issue. After that he accepted that they watched the local news, though he often said it was boring. Nothing about Carmen O'Keefe ever appeared.

They kept a watch on the field too. From the window of Annie's bedroom they could see across the field to the little wood and the supermarket. If the police descended on the grave, or anyone else began digging there, they could see it, or, if they were at school, could see the results. No one ever did. No one ever went near the grave, except sheep. As the days slipped by everything became deceptively normal. They got up, dressed Jamie, had breakfast, went to school and covered up their real situation just as they had before. Apart from the fact that they could be less obsessive about locking doors, nothing had changed. Many years later, when they were back in the house for a death, Matthew tried to put their feelings into words.

'It was as if you'd just had your first *you know*, and then the two of you had just got up and walked away like nothing had happened.'

'Don't talk like that,' said Annie, bending over her knitting. 'You know I don't like it.'

At the time, of course, no such formulation would have been possible, and they confined themselves to talking, late at night, about why there had been no public fuss.

'Perhaps she was going away anyway,' said Matthew. 'So they just assume she's gone where she said she was going.'

'Where could she have been on her way to, in our back garden?' asked Annie. 'And she had no luggage or anything.'

Matthew had to concede this.

'Perhaps her husband had been half expecting her to do a bunk with one of her boyfriends,' he tried again. 'And when she disappeared he just assumed that was what she had done. Or perhaps he told the police and they just decided she was the sort of woman who *does* just take herself off.'

'That's more likely,' admitted Annie. 'But even more likely is that he did it, and now he's telling everybody that's what she's done.'

That, agreed Matthew, was true. But the fact was, they didn't know. Soon it became eerie. Matthew thought about it often, lying awake in bed at night. They had found a body, a murdered body, in their back garden, and they had buried it. Yet the woman's disappearance was apparently a matter of not the least concern to anyone: there was no newspaper publicity, no police investigation. It was as if the body had never been there at all. If it had not been for the dirt on his duffel coat and shirt, a clump of earth clinging to the spade, the old door still against the garage wall, Matthew might have been tempted to regard it all as a dream. When, two weeks after the burial, they found a new but broken torch in a flowerbed at the back, they were at first excited. It was a clue, Annie said. But after thinking about it, Matthew pointed out it could have been thrown over by a neighbour, or from the field which abutted the house. It was really nothing very much.

In the end the vacuum became intolerable.

'We've got to find out!' Matthew said to Annie, on their way to school. 'We've got to find out what people are saying about Mrs O'Keefe.'

'What should we do? Go to church again?'

'It could begin to look suspicious, if we start pumping people every time we go there about Mrs O'Keefe. We must try to think of something else.'

So they took thought and nattered, and they had almost decided that Annie should try to have some dressmaking lessons from an elderly, loose-tongued member of the St Joseph's congregation ('It would be a good idea, anyway,' said Annie, a born home-maker; 'it would be so useful'), when an alternative possibility dropped on to the doormat as part of their meagre mail. It was Matthew who opened it.

'An invitation to a children's summer party at the Irish

Club,' he said, his eyes speculative. 'A lot of adults are always around at those. Parents and grandparents and that.'

'Who do you think should go?' asked Annie.

'You. You're good at getting the gossip.'

'Why don't we all go? We could say that we're giving Dad a rest.'

'I want to go!' shouted Greg, and Jamie joined in without knowing at all what he was demanding to go to.

'All right, we'll all go,' said Matthew. 'I'll keep my eye on the kids while you . . .'

'But you're the elder,' objected Annie. 'They'll talk more openly to you.'

'No, they won't. I keep letting slip that I know something was going on involving Dad. That's what made Harry Curtin wary. You can go along and just look sweet and listen.'

The party was in ten days' time, on a Saturday in the early evening. It turned out to be a fine June day, and Greg and Jamie were high on excited anticipation all day long. Getting to the club didn't present any problems. They all took the bus into town and then the bus to Temple Newsam that went along the York Road. There were no problems about leaving their father, of course. He was left alone every weekday when they were at school. It was like leaving an old dog in the house that they knew would not get up to anything.

When they got off the bus, they had to cross the York Road by one of the iron bridges that spanned the busy road. This was an adventure for Greg, but Jamie was frightened by the roar of the traffic going in both directions under them. Once they were safely on the right side they quietened him with the prospect of the cakes and sweets and pop he could expect at the party. Irish Club children's parties were lavish in their provision of tuck. When they got to the club and went into the big room beside the bar they were greeted heartily by all the adults officiating.

'Annie! Matthew! And who are these? Gregory and Jamie, is it? It's good to see you. Where's your dad? Did he bring you?'

'No, we came by bus,' they said, telling the truth in case

they had been seen getting off it. 'To give Dad more time to himself.'

'I'll bet he can do with it. Is he coping all right? Sure and you four children must be a full-time job.'

'Oh, we are. He doesn't get many free moments. That's why we wanted to come today.'

Everyone nodded and accepted that, and they began mingling in. Matthew found that, once the party started, he was treated as a kind of honorary adult. It wasn't thought that he was in need of sandwiches or sticky buns, but he was pressed into service to see that the others were well supplied. When the party games and races outside began he was made an umpire. It wasn't as though he was the oldest there. Somehow, without knowing of their father's condition, the adults seemed to sense that he was head of his family. It was an odd feeling, at once pleasing and frightening. Matthew felt, as he had felt before, that he had been ejected prematurely out of childhood.

Annie did not find her task as easy as Matthew had forecast. A girl of twelve wandering round among the adults and listening to their conversation quite soon gets herself noticed. The bar and the other rooms around the club had plenty of groups of adults chatting happily, though there was little serious drinking going on as yet. Annie got herself a plate laden with children's party fodder and walked through the rooms apparently purposefully, really looking for likely gossip sessions. The trouble was that when any hard core gossip was going ahead, the talkers tended to bend forwards and talk low, and it was impossible to sit near enough to overhear. It was only after wandering around with her plate for ten minutes or so that Annie managed to hear something that made her prick up her ears.

'Oh, yes – gone. Just walked out of the house without so much as a goodbye.'

It was Gladys Harcourt, the woman whom Annie had hoped might give her dressmaking lessons. She was tucking into cakes and pastries with Miss Porter from St Joseph's, and they were blessedly oblivious to their surroundings and had not switched to hushed tones. Annie surveyed the lie of the land and picked on a chair near, but slightly behind them. Then she tucked into her food as though that were her only interest.

'Mind you, you couldn't say it was unexpected,' said Miss Porter, with relish. 'Even by that dim husband of hers, from what I hear.'

'Maybe not. Though by all accounts he was pretty shocked that she just took off like that.'

'Left all her clothes and everything behind, so they say. *That*'s not like Carmen O'Keefe.'

'I should think she's found someone who'll provide. Off with the old and on with the new – clothes as well as men.'

'Has anyone any idea who it is?'

'There's been names mentioned,' said Mrs Harcourt wistfully. 'But then they turn up at church and everything seems normal. Mind you, I never thought it could be anyone we'd be likely to know. I'd guess it's someone in a different league financially to any of the men at St Joseph's. Always in the past she's had pretty – well – pretty basic men, if you get my meaning. You knew what she wanted them for. When she got someone with plenty of the ready, she seized the opportunity with both hands.'

'Rob was home, wasn't he?'

'Oh yes. And his mother was visiting.'

'Couldn't that be why she took off without her things – to avoid a big row?'

'I suppose so,' said Mrs Harcourt, pursing her lips in a sceptical moue. 'Mind you, they don't know that she took *none* of her things, because neither of them knows what she had . . . I wouldn't have thought Carmen was one to avoid a good dust-up, though. Rather enjoyed them, as a rule.'

'Still, if she was sure she was wiping the dust of Leeds off her feet, she might not have thought it worthwhile having a fuss. So it could be one of her usual type of men.'

'Meaning beefy, not too bright, wanting a good time, or just wanting plain good old you-know-what.'

'There have been enough of those in the past – some of them from our congregation, I'm afraid. And a number from this club too!'

'I suppose we all know some of the names –'

Annie's heart thumped as they went through them.

'I should think we do! Brian Curtis, Rory O'Rourke, Vincent Maddigan, Dermot Heenan, Paul Mackenzie –'

'Right!' said Mrs Harcourt. 'Most of them didn't make much secret of it. Dermot Heenan was cannier about it, but then he's a good family man.'

'Poor soul, with all those bairns to look after. He's doing penance if any man is. But some of the others –'

'Blatant! But what I'm not sure about is who she'd been going with recently.'

'Apart from Heenan, you mean?'

'Yes, apart from him.'

Miss Porter put up two fingers.

'Jim Leary and Andy Patterson.' Then she put up a third. 'And there was a bit of talk about Kevin Holmes, but I don't know if there was anything in it.'

Annie memorized the names. Jim Leary and Kevin Holmes were vaguely known to her.

'Pretty much her usual types,' said Mrs Harcourt. 'Any of them been seen at St Joseph's recently?'

'Not that I know of. Or was Jim Leary there a while back? But anyway, none of them are great churchgoers. You'd be more likely to see them here . . . Of course, there's something you've got to remember –'

'What?'

'She had money herself – had had since her mother died earlier this year. So she could have taken off with any one of her navvy types and they're blueing *her* money on a binge.'

Mrs Harcourt considered that carefully, munching flaky pastry and licking the remnants from her lips.

'Hmmm. It's possible, but I can't see it. You don't know her well, do you?'

'No. Of her, of course.'

'She's a hard, calculating bitch of a woman, pardon my language. Eye on the main chance and eager for any quick buck there may be around.' She shook her head. 'Oh no, she'll not be paying for her pleasures if there's any other way of getting them. Careful – there's Mrs O'Keefe!'

Annie nearly jumped out of her skin. An image flashed through her mind of the body in the bloody yellow blouse – here, at the party, like Banquo in the play. Fearful she had drawn attention to herself, she started towards the room where the children's party was, but she heard a whispered, 'How long's she been there?' and then a call of, 'Annie, love – how are you? It's a long time since I saw you.'

She turned reluctantly and went towards them.

'Oh, Annie and I have seen each other not long since,' said Miss Porter. 'Had tea together, didn't we, after church? Been having a quiet eat, have you?'

'No, I'm just on my way back to the party,' said Annie.

'People say you're coping very well, you and your dad,' said Mrs Harcourt. 'Is there anything I could do? I'd be only too happy to come round –'

'Well, there is something,' said Annie, her heart still beating disturbingly. 'There's no need to come round – Dad's coping wonderfully, and we all chip in and help – but I did wonder if you could give me a few dressmaking lessons. Quite elementary things – darning, mending and that. Mum taught me to do them, but I'm not really very good. And children's clothes seem so expensive. If I picked up things quickly, perhaps I could learn how to make simple things for Jamie.'

'Annie, love, I'd be delighted . . . Hello, Mrs O'Keefe! Glad you're still here. Enjoying the party?'

Annie turned, her reluctance almost palpable, to see a comfortably-built elderly woman, with grey hair turning white, a friendly smile and sad eyes. She was dressed in old-fashioned fawns and browns with sturdy brogue shoes and thick stockings.

'I'm still here, more's the pity. Helping that great lump of a son of mine. He's still at sixes and sevens, poor lad.'

Her accent was warm and Irish; one that Annie was used to and found comforting.

'Still not got over it yet?' asked Miss Porter.

'Not entirely, though sure it's what I expected all along. And it's what anyone should expect if they marry a . . . a

83

woman of that type – and I nearly used a word I shouldn't, and I wouldn't want to use with a child around!'

'You never had any idea she'd take off like that?' asked Mrs Harcourt. Mrs O'Keefe considered.

'Well, she was always what you might call restless. Or there are nastier words that describe it better. Even when I was in the same house she was hard put to hide it. Always on the look out for . . . well, let's say excitement, for cheap thrills. So when she just took off I was surprised, but then I was *not* surprised, if you take my meaning.'

'You never had any doubts she'd gone off with a man?'

Mrs O'Keefe raised her eyebrows eloquently.

'Lord above, no! Did you know Carmen? If you did, you'll not be doubting she went off with something in trousers.'

'It must have been an awful shock for your Rob.'

Mrs O'Keefe pondered.

'Well, it was a shock, to be sure, but I'll not say it ought to have been, and I'll not say it was awful. To my way of thinking, he's the better for her going, and the Fathers can say what they like about the sanctity of marriage, and I'd agree with them, but what's a man to do if his wife hasn't the first notion of honouring it? No, it was a terrible shock, but he'll get over it. Men are great babies, aren't they? They cry when they lose their lollies, but they're a whole lot better off without them more often than not.'

'He'll be back on the rig soon, won't he?'

'Yes, he will. Maybe that'll help. Give him time to think. If he sees it aright, he'll realize she's no great loss.'

'You'll be wanting to see how the little ones are doing,' said Miss Porter, turning to Annie with a smile, but clearly wanting to have the sort of no-holds-barred gossip that her presence was preventing.

'I suppose I'd better. Matthew's with them though.' Annie tried not to seem reluctant.

'Annie lost her mother some months ago,' said Mrs Harcourt. She cast a meaningful glance which Annie intercepted at Mrs O'Keefe. 'Ellen Heenan.'

Mrs O'Keefe immediately turned to her with a look of concern and special interest.

'Oh dear, how sad. I knew her. Sure and she was a good woman, and she'll be a great loss to you all. How are you doing?'

'Oh, we're all fine,' said Annie. Then, conscious she shouldn't minimize their loss, she added: 'We miss her, though.'

'You will be doing. Is your dad coping well?'

'Oh, quite well. But there's a lot for him to learn.'

Annie felt Mrs O'Keefe's eyes on her, and shifted from foot to foot.

'But your mother will have taught you to do most things, won't she?'

'Oh yes, there's a lot I can do.'

'It's better than being split up, isn't it?'

'Nobody's going to split us up!' said Annie fiercely.

'That's right,' said Mrs O'Keefe, nodding agreement. 'Now, is there anything I can do for you?'

'Are you not going back to Ireland yet awhile?' asked Miss Porter.

'It can't be too soon for me,' she replied. 'My Rob feels at home here, but I never will. But I want to do one or two things for him before I go. Get one of those deep freezer things and cook some meals for him so there'll be plenty for him to eat when next he comes home. Men are helpless creatures, God knows, though maybe it's us that make them so. I could do some cooking for you at the same time,' she added, turning back to Annie.

'Oh, there's no need,' she said. 'We've three cooks in the house – Dad, Matthew and me.'

'Then it's lucky you are. I should have trained my Rob –'

'He may find a woman-friend to look after him,' put in Mrs Harcourt, consciously daring. 'A fine chap like your Rob doesn't like being alone.'

'Well, it'd be sin, and contrary to what I believe in and what I taught him. Having once chosen Carmen he'd be better off not choosing a second time. The world's changing, even in Ireland, but as far as I'm concerned, it's not changing for the better . . . People haven't the same conscience about what they do . . .'

It was a thought that remained with Annie after she had slipped away, and for long after. Standards were crumbling, people were doing whatever they wanted to, without thought for what was right, or for what the effects on others would be. She didn't have to look outside her own home to be convinced of the truth of Mrs O'Keefe's remarks. They became something she tried to live her life by, and something she remembered when she and Matthew came back to the house in Calverley Row fourteen years later.

CHAPTER 9

A Visitor

All the children were pleased they had gone to the summer party. For the two smallest it was a change, a meeting with other children who were not school or playschool friends. For the two eldest it provided answers to some of their questions, as well as pointing towards some potentially useful avenues of inquiry – if they should decide to start going up them.

'We learnt one or two things,' said Matthew. 'We know that on the Sunday evening she disappeared, and her husband and mother-in-law immediately assumed she'd run off with a man.'

'Or just pretended to believe that,' Annie pointed out. 'I mean, he's apparently very upset, or so he makes out. But would you be, if you were married to her, and she was going with all those other men?'

'I don't know,' said Matthew, after consideration. 'It's something we don't really know about, isn't it? He is a Catholic, even if he hardly ever comes to church. For us, marriage is for life, so he could be upset because he won't have any other chance to have children and that.'

'Maybe,' said Annie, thoughtful too, and conscious of their inexperience. 'I wish we could meet him and find out what he's like.'

'Not very bright, from what you say. But that doesn't mean he couldn't feel very jealous . . . Still, we mustn't forget the other men in her life. They could have been jealous too.'

'Particularly if they'd been cut out by someone else richer than them ready to whisk her off with him.'

Matthew nodded, then was struck by a thought.

'He wasn't necessarily ready to do that. That's what they think, because she's suddenly disappeared. We *know* she didn't go anywhere.'

'Yes, *we* know that. And so does the murderer . . . What about those names? Jim Leary, Andy Patterson and Kevin Holmes. I think Jim Leary is the father of Sally Leary in my year at school. And there's her brother, Peter Leary, in fifth year. I don't know anything about their father, or what he works at.'

'Yes, I think that's the family. And Kevin Holmes has that small garage and workshop somewhere in Stanningley. Dad took the car there once or twice, but he said he wasn't very good. He said using fellow-Catholics had its limits.'

'Has he got any children?'

'Don't know. There's a Holmes in fourth year, but I'm not sure that he's his. What about Andy Patterson?'

'Never heard of him. Doesn't ring any bells at all.'

'Could he be the rich one, do you think?'

'I don't think so. They obviously knew him, Mrs Harcourt and Miss Porter, and they didn't count him as rich. They thought the rich one was somebody unknown – not a member of the congregation or the Irish Club.'

Matthew thought.

'There's no need for there to be a rich one at all. They just assume there is one, like I say, one who whisked her away. But she wasn't whisked. There's no need for there to have been any new boyfriend at all.'

Annie thought a bit about this.

'So what are you saying?'

'That we'd better concentrate on the ones we do know about. The three they mentioned.'

'And we've got to remember that even those are just possibilities. They don't *know*.'

'Still, we can ask a few questions,' said Matthew.

'Yes. We could talk to the Leary children,' said Annie. 'Find out if their dad's been up to anything.'

'How do you ask someone if their dad's been up to anything?' asked Matthew. Annie nodded agreement. It wasn't going to be easy. 'You've got to be very careful,' Matthew went on. 'I don't think you should ask questions at all. The more questions we ask about Mrs O'Keefe, the more people might wonder about her. Maybe it would be better just to keep quiet.'

'Except that it's so awful, not knowing,' said Annie.

'Nobody knows. They're just spec – just guessing. But it would be good if we could overhear people talking, like you did yesterday, rather than asking questions.'

Annie shook her head. 'I don't think kids do talk about their father having affairs with other women,' she said. 'They just sort of bottle it up. I'd *hate* to talk to other people about our dad and *that woman*. I'd feel dirty.'

'Then we'll have to be really clever,' said Matthew. 'Dead cunning.'

But Annie didn't find it all that easy to be dead cunning next day at school. Dead cunning wasn't really in her nature. It was a fine day, and there was lots going on in the playground at break times. During the dinner hour, she located Sally Leary, sitting by the bicycle shed, but she wasn't alone: there were two of her best friends with her. It just didn't seem natural to Annie to go over and talk to them, because she wasn't one of that group: she knew them, but she wasn't one of them. They kept together throughout the break, eating their sandwiches, talking, giggling. As luck would have it, though, when the bell rang for afternoon classes they separated, and Annie could come up beside Sally Leary in the corridor.

'Didn't see you at the Irish Club party on Saturday,' she said, she hoped casually. 'Were you there?'

Sally was a pretty little thing, with soft fair hair that seemed tinged with red.

'No, none of us wanted to go,' she said, readily enough. 'It was our Peter's birthday, and some of his mates were coming round.'

'You should have come. It was really good.'

'My mum doesn't like the Irish Club. She doesn't like Dad going there – he gets drinking and that.'

Annie would dearly have liked to know what 'and that'

covered, but probably Sally had only the vaguest idea herself.

'Don't suppose that stops your dad going,' she said.

'Oh, he still goes. But not as much as he did.'

She was certainly talking as if her father was still at home. But then they knew nobody had run off with Carmen O'Keefe – Annie had to keep telling herself that. What was interesting was what, if anything, had happened between Jim Leary and her before her disappearance – a word she now preferred to use to 'death', even to herself.

'Our dad used to go to the club a lot when Mother was pregnant,' she said. 'He doesn't have the time now.'

Sally Leary shot her a glance, but then they had to separate to go off to different classes. As she got together her books and pens, Annie pondered that glance. Did it just say that Sally Leary had heard rumours about their father during their mother's pregnancy? Or was there something more – something like fellow-feeling? Was she indicating that both their fathers had had a fancy woman in common? Annie thought it just possible she had been trying to say that. When she told Matthew about the exchange that evening, she said: 'I think I'll sort of hang around. In case she wants to talk about it. You could do the same with Peter Leary.'

'Peter Leary's three years older than me. I've never talked to him – not *talked* – in my life.'

'He and his mates hang around the corner shop after school – they keep an eye on the kids for Mr Patel, to stop them shoplifting. You could talk to him there.'

'I don't think he'd be interested in talking to me. He'd think I was just a kid.'

But Matthew was wrong. The Leary children did want to talk to the Heenan children, and they signified their wish by the usual signs and symbols of childhood. When Matthew went into Mr Patel's corner supermarket – it was two small shops knocked together, and operating on a self-serve basis – he saw Peter Leary and one or two of his friends strolling up and down the aisles. He and Peter not only registered each other, but each was aware that the other had done so. Matthew wandered around trying to decide what he could plausibly buy, and finally decided on two tins of corned beef that they could have for tea one day with salad or chips. The tinned meat section was situated conveniently close to where Peter Leary was standing. He was a lanky boy, his school uniform worn with a sort of casual flair, a lock of brown hair falling over his left eye. From the eyes there came a definite glint of intelligence, or at least sharpness.

'Is it true you keep a watchout for shoplifters?' Matthew asked him. Like Annie, he put on a show of casualness as part of the performance.

'Yeah,' responded Peter, much more readily than a six-teen-year-old would normally respond to a thirteen-year-old, and thus giving Matthew one more sign. 'You get to know who they are. I didn't suspect you, by the way.'

'I never have yet. Does he pay you?'

'In sweets and pop and that. Cigarettes, if you want, but only tens. The busy period's over now. Are you walking down the road?'

Matthew knew then for certain that he wanted to talk. He nodded and smiled.

'Yes. I'll just pay for these.'

Peter waited while he paid for the tins. As they went out of the shop and began the walk in the direction of both their houses Peter said: 'It must be difficult managing, with your dad not working.'

'Oh, it's not that bad. There's various allowances and extras you can get, with him having to stay home and look after us. From the Social Security office, I mean.'

'Yes, I suppose he can't take a job or . . . get out much.'

'No, not now.'

'There were . . . stories about your dad a while back.'

So it was out into the open! Matthew put in his penn'orth.

'There were about your dad too.'

'Were the ones about your dad true?' asked Peter Leary.

'I don't know. I mean, we don't *know*, for certain. You see, we never heard any gossip at the time, while Mum was still alive. We only heard it after she died. So we can't go along and ask Dad about it, just like that. And there's nobody else to ask. But I think it's true.'

'What makes you think that?'

'Because he was always talking about doing overtime — that's why he was out of the house so much. But there's a recession on. People are being laid off, like Dad himself was eventually. His boss practically told me there wasn't any overtime for him to do . . . Was there a lot of gossip?'

'No, there wasn't much. Less than usual with *her*.'

'Is that what you call her?'

'Yes.'

'We call her *that woman*.'

They exchanged glances of understanding and sympathy.

'I think your dad and her were a bit discreet. Perhaps your dad was a bit ashamed, with your mum being pregnant, and some of you very young . . . Not like our dad.'

'Was he open about it?'

Peter thought, his face flecked with bitterness.

'Well, he didn't *flaunt* it, like some do. But he didn't keep it quiet either. They were seen quite openly together. Mum was going off her head. Thought she was going to be left with all of us on her hands. I had to talk to Dad.'

'Did you?' said Matthew admiringly. 'I don't think I could do that. What did he say?'

'Got all stroppy at first. I just looked at him — sort of with contempt. It worked, in a way. He tried this man-to-man thing, saying it was just a bit of a fling, that a man had to break out from time to time, that it wasn't serious, and it wouldn't last. Said I'd understand when I was a bit older.'

'When was all this?'

'Last summer. August–September time. I think your dad may have been next in line, though there weren't any whispers till towards Christmas, so far as I remember. Like I said, he was cleverer about it . . .' The boy's feelings suddenly erupted. 'It was disgusting with my dad, with everyone talking behind their backs about him and *her*.'

'Did your dad really break it off with her?'

Peter Leary grimaced.

'That's the question, isn't it? I don't know. He could have . . . gone with her now and then. In the fire service you work funny hours, and there are all sorts of emergencies . . . He and Mum rub along, but it's not very nice at home.'

'What about *her*?'

'I don't give a fuck about *her*!' said Peter Leary violently. 'They say she's run off with someone. I hope he treats her like dirt, because that's what she is.'

'Yes, she is . . . We've heard several names of men who've been with her,' said Matthew, though he suspected Peter Leary would have heard them. 'But some of them have been to church with their families since she disappeared, so she hasn't run off with them.'

'One of those will be Dad,' said Peter Leary, with a twisted reminiscent smile. 'Mum insisted that he went to confession and then came to Mass with us. He said that was just daft superstition, but he did it . . . Who were the other two?'

'Well, there's Kevin Holmes and Andy Patterson. I don't know Andy Patterson at all.'

'He has a small electrical shop in Bramley. I heard his name too. I don't think he's married.'

'Does your mum have any idea where she's gone, or who she went with?'

'No. Just says, "Good riddance to bad rubbish."'

'Well,' said Matthew, falsely cheerful, 'at least she's gone now. No danger any longer.'

'If she *has* gone.'

Matthew's heart thumped dangerously.

'What do you mean?'

'Town the size of Leeds, she could be anywhere,' explained Peter. 'Chapeltown, Menston, Seaforth. She could be just a short car trip away. This is my turn-off. Keep in touch.'

'Yes, I will . . . Tell me if you hear anything.'

'That's what I mean.'

The conversation with Peter Leary cheered Matthew up: it made him feel less lonely. There was someone else who hated Carmen O'Keefe, and for the same reason; someone else who would like to know exactly what she'd been doing and who she'd been sleeping with in her last months. Only Peter did not know they were her last months, of course. Matthew wished he could have told him she was dead; it would have been a seal on their new relationship, and in retrospect he felt a bit inclined to boast about what he had achieved on the night of her murder. But he realized he could not confide in someone he knew so little. That part of the secret had to remain locked between him and Annie.

At home things remained pretty much as they had been. On bad days communication with their father was virtually non-existent: he would emit a noise somewhere between a grunt and a whine, and it was impossible to know whether what they said to him got through. He had better days too, but they were few. They put away from them the thought that one day they would have to call a doctor to him. They *wouldn't*, and that was that. As soon as they got away from that pathetic incubus, though, they were becoming more carefree: they knew they could cope. It was hard work, but they could cope. There were now no threats that they could see to their security. Money came in regularly, and it was adequate to their needs (the fact that their father ate very little, and neither drank nor smoked helped a lot). They put money aside for gas, electricity, rates and for any expenses they had not calculated for. The smaller ones talked about their mother no longer – nor about their father, if they could avoid it. They accepted Matthew and Annie as a sort of tandem replacement for both.

On the Saturday after his conversation with Peter Leary, it was Matthew's turn to do the washing. Keeping the little ones neat and tidy for school meant there was a great deal of washing. While Matthew sorted out the loads for the machine and humped them downstairs from the linen basket in the bathroom, Annie played with Greg and Jamie outside on the back lawn. The party at the Irish Club had stimulated their taste for races and outdoor games. They played hide-and-seek, and then they ran egg-and-spoon races. Around half-past five Matthew's wash was done, and he went out into the garden.

'What shall we have for tea?' he shouted over the laughter.

'Fish and chips!' yelled Greg.

'Yes, fish and chips,' echoed Jamie.

'Shall we?' asked Matthew of Annie. 'There's enough money.'

'All right, for once. The sausages will keep.'

So Matthew walked across the bypass and down to the little Rodley fish and chip shop. There was quite a crowd there, and it took him a while to get served (being smallish didn't help). He bought four portions of cod and four of chips (Gregory and Jamie shared one), and then he started off back home with the deliciously warm bundle cradled in his arms. When he got back to Calverley Row he ran round to the back garden, where the fun and games were still in progress.

'Come on! Fish and chips up!' he called.

The children ran up to him, shouting enthusiastically, and Annie followed behind. Matthew opened the kitchen door, but then he stood in the doorway transfixed. Sitting at the kitchen table was an elderly woman with a kindly smile, dressed in rather dull clothes and looking at them penetratingly. In front of her was a dark round fruit-cake on a plate.

'Well now,' she said. 'You children have been having people on, haven't you?'

CHAPTER 10

A Way Out

'What are you doing here?' Matthew demanded, when he had got his breath back.

The woman smiled gently. She seemed very unmenacing.

'I came to bring you round this cake. I thought I might as well make one for you, since I was making one for my Rob.'

'Rob?' said Matthew, his voice cracking.

'O'Keefe. I'm his mother. Your sister there knows me, don't you, Annie?'

'Yes,' said Annie, in a whisper of a voice.

'And you're Matthew, aren't you?' She smiled the smile of one who is used to talking to children, and enjoys it. 'I hear you helped out wonderfully at the party. Anyway, I saw you all playing happily out there at the back, so I thought: "I'll just leave it for them in the house."'

'You've no right –'

'Sure, everyone's in and out of each other's houses in Ireland, Matthew. Did your mother never tell you that? Is that fish and chips you have there? You'll not want it to be getting cold. Is that your tea?'

'Yes – we don't have it often,' said Annie, feeling oddly on the defensive.

The woman's smile was still encouragingly ordinary.

'Nothing wrong with fish and chips now and again. But you should eat it off plates, not out of paper with your fingers like heathens. Was that what you were going to do? I'll bet your mother wouldn't have wanted you doing that. Where are the plates, now, and the knives and forks?'

She bustled round at their direction, put plates around the

kitchen table, then knives and forks. Finally she took the bundle from Matthew and started sharing it out. The four children watched her, a feeling of impending disaster not yet banished from the older ones' stomachs, in spite of the woman's good humour and air of warmth.

'There we are then. A meal fit for a king. Sit down and eat it while it's still warm.'

They all sat down, but as she started in on the fish with her unaccustomed knife and fork Annie said:

'Thank you very much for the cake. We'll like that very much. You don't have to stay.'

It sounded very rude, but the woman showed no sign of having taken offence.

'Oh, I think I do,' she said, shaking her head sadly. 'You see, I've been upstairs.'

In that moment their world shattered around them. Then they knew for sure. But the two smallest children went on eating hungrily, quite unconscious.

'You'd no right!' said Matthew, more confidently this time.

'No, I hadn't, I admit. But you see, I called up, and all the reply I got was a sort of grunting sound. I thought someone must be ill. Now eat up and we'll discuss it afterwards.' She sat down and looked at them: plump, comfortable and motherly. 'I'm not here to harm you, you know. But we've got to think what's best for you all.'

They ate up with the best will they could muster. When they were finished, Mrs O'Keefe took the plates to the sink and began to wash them up.

'It's still nice and sunny outside,' she said. 'Why don't the young ones go out again to play?'

Greg and Jamie were very willing, and as she watched them in the garden, Mrs O'Keefe inquired about their ages and names, and what their characters were. 'I love little ones,' she said. Matthew and Annie dried the plates and cutlery, and then, so naturally that nothing needed to be said, they all sat down again at the kitchen table and looked at each other.

'How long has he been like that?' asked Mrs O'Keefe.

'Oh, he's ill,' said Annie quickly. 'Just a few days. He'll get better.'

Mrs O'Keefe looked reproachful and shook her head.

'Annie, love, I'm not a great brain but I've seen a bit of life and I know that a man doesn't get to that state in a few days. I want to help you, child, but I can do nothing if all you do is tell me lies.'

The two children looked at each other. They had grown so close to each other in the last few months that normally they would have known instinctively what the other wanted to do. But this situation was unheard-of, unforeseen, so that now they were uncertain. Lying was endemic to them, and it needed a great shift in attitude to start telling the truth. Annie looked down at the table, leaving the decision to her brother.

'Since Mother died,' said Matthew at last. Mrs O'Keefe's face was fused with an emotion she could not suppress.

'You poor children!' she said.

'The ambulance people brought him home, and he just seemed – well, almost knocked out. He kept talking about being punished and that, and didn't want to eat, or go out . . .'

'And things have gone from bad to worse since then?'

'Yes.'

'Why did you tell no one?'

'We were afraid to. You see, we thought they'd decide to take us into care.'

'Sure and you could do with a bit of care!'

'No! We're a family! We want to stay together. And me and Annie can manage. We have done for months now.'

'Please go away and leave us alone!' pleaded Annie. 'And don't tell anyone about us either. We're all right. You can see the little ones are all right.'

Mrs O'Keefe leaned forward over the table.

'But your father: is he all right?'

They looked at her defensively.

'But there's nothing we can do about him,' said Matthew. 'That's just how he is. We make sure he eats and washes and changes his clothes.'

Mrs O'Keefe shook her head in reproof.

'Are you sure nobody else can do anything for him? And if you'd got help earlier, don't you think there'd be a better chance of getting him normal again?'

They looked down at the table. It was something that they had barely considered, had subconsciously decided to put out of their minds.

'I did say he ought to see a doctor,' said Matthew, looking down at the table.

'But you did nothing about it. He needs a doctor, he needs a priest, he needs a psychiatrist, if we can find one that's halfway sensible. He needs all sorts of things, your dad, but he's not getting them, is he?'

There was silence.

'No,' said Annie at last.

But Matthew resisted the guilt she was trying to thrust on him.

'He deserved it!' he cried passionately. 'After what he did to Mum when she was ill.'

'And is that for you to judge, child? Sure, you're talking as if you were God – at thirteen! What you mean is he . . . went with my daughter-in-law, isn't it?'

'Yes.'

'If you condemned to madness all the men who've been with Carmen, the country's asylums would be full to bursting! Men are weak creatures – you'll be weak yourself when you grow up, Matthew – and she threw out her nets and trapped them one after another. But the affairs never lasted long, and they mostly went back to their families in the end. It's her you should blame, more than the men.'

After a moment's thought Matthew said: 'If she just . . . had them for a bit then chucked them aside, why did she come round here after him?'

'I don't know, Matthew,' said Mrs O'Keefe, shaking her head. 'Maybe she hadn't quite finished with him, maybe it was a bit more serious than the others. Maybe it was always the men who got tired and threw her aside. I don't know anything about her love affairs – "love"! What a word! – and I don't want to. I can't explain what Carmen might do: she's a woman with no morals and no scruples – I'll make no bones about that! If she wants something, even if it's someone else's, she just goes after it.'

'She's horrible!' said Annie, passionately, but remembering to talk about her as if she was still alive.

'I'll not quarrel with that. And my Rob's better off without her – even he is beginning to see that.'

The mention of her son brought back to Matthew's mind the whole question of who had murdered her.

'Does anyone know where she's gone?' he asked cunningly.

'Not an idea in the world,' said Mrs O'Keefe, with a wave of her hand. 'No one's seen her and no one's heard from her. The police have had no news of her, and to tell you the truth they're not very interested, because they know from me the type of woman she is. It's good riddance, say I.'

'Because someone said the other day that she could still be in Leeds,' said Matthew. 'She could be in some suburb on the other side of the city.'

'I'd be willing to bet someone would have seen her if so. She isn't one to sit at home slaving over a sink, not Carmen: she's always out and about. My bet is that she'll have found herself some businessman who wants a good time, God help him, and she'll be in Manchester or Birmingham or somewhere like that.'

'I expect you're right,' said Annie solemnly.

'Now, we're getting off the subject. It's neither here nor there who Carmen has gone off with, nor where she is. The question is: what are we going to do?'

'I don't see why you have to do anything,' said Annie bitterly. 'We're all right as we are. You can see the young ones have been properly fed and kept clean and tidy.'

'Annie, love, your father needs attention,' said Mrs O'Keefe, summoning up all her peasant common sense against this childish irrationality. 'Medical attention. No doctor in the world is going to let things go on as they are.' She looked at the girl and then said gently: 'You'd have been found out before summer was over, you know. Summer's the time when you expect to see people. The neighbours would have started wondering about your father before long. Eventually the little ones would have talked — maybe they have already, but people haven't quite caught on. And before long your father was bound to be ill — physically ill — and then you'd have had to call a doctor.'

'But we don't want to be taken into care!' said Matthew passionately. 'Just separated and handed over to this family and that one.'

'And did I say anything about that?' demanded Mrs O'Keefe. 'Sure, I never did. Now, the first thing is to get the doctor to your dad. We need to know how bad the poor fellow is, and what the chances are that he might recover. That'll be for Monday morning. But whatever happens, it's going to be a long process. The best thing is for me to move in now —'

'You?'

'I don't see any alternative. The doctor will want to know there's someone looking after you. I think we'd better conjure up some kind of story —'

She looked at the two solemn childish faces opposite her, seriously thinking as they took in the new situation.

'We invented an Auntie Maureen,' said Annie. 'For *her*. We said she was here on a visit from Ireland. And we talked about her to one or two other people — so that they thought there was someone in the family taking an interest.'

'Well, I can't suddenly become a Maureen,' said Mrs O'Keefe briskly. 'People know me here, and know that I'm a Constance. But I can say your Auntie Maureen is a friend of mine in Ireland, and that she phoned me to come round and see that you were all right.'

'What will you say about Dad?' Matthew asked.

'We'd better not tell the truth, had we? Make you children a nine days' wonder at St Joseph's. I think we could say that all the work and worry and responsibility finally got to him and he's had some kind of nervous breakdown.'

'Yes!' said the children. 'Like it was recent.'

'That's it. But I'm not sure that will wash with the doctor. I'd better stay closer to the truth with him, but tell him that I'm here indefinitely to look after you all. Nobody's going to come rushing round to take you all into care, you know. It's a last resort.'

'Are you sure?' asked Annie.

'Oh, yes. No question,' she said, slowly and explicitly: 'I'll not *let* you be taken into care.'

It was very comforting – the most wonderful relief. Annie and Matthew looked at each other, and smiled.

'How shall we manage about bedrooms?' asked Matthew.

'Well, we'll have to manage, won't we? Perhaps we'd better not make any changes for tonight – the little ones won't want too many strange things happening at once. Is there a good sofa anywhere?'

'There's one in the sitting room. And there's an old sofa-bed in the dining room, that used to be Aunt Lucy's.'

'You have some relatives, then?'

'No, she's dead,' said Matthew. 'She left us this house. All the relatives we have are Mum's in Ireland, and they don't care, though they pretend to.'

'Well, let's have a look at that sofa-bed, then – just for tonight. Then I'll ring my Rob and tell him I'll not be home. Maybe you can find me an old nightie of your mother's.'

So that was how things sorted themselves out. They pulled the old sofa out to make a bed for her, sneezing at the dust that months of neglect had allowed to accumulate. 'We'll have a good hoover round tomorrow,' said Mrs O'Keefe. Then they fetched sheets and blankets and pillows down from the airing cupboard upstairs. They got Greg and Jamie in from the garden, and Mrs O'Keefe took them upstairs to wash them and put them to bed. When they were in their pyjamas she told them to say good night to their father. She stood behind them in the doorway as – reluctantly – they did so, getting no more than a grunt in reply. Dermot Heenan looked at Mrs O'Keefe without comment or curiosity and, confused, she shut the door and shooed the children to their room.

It seemed odd to Matthew and Annie not to have the children to put to bed. When they were settled and Mrs O'Keefe came down again, she saw at once that they were at a loose end.

'I bet your school work will have suffered with all this,' she said. 'We'd better make that first priority over the summer: catching up. And you'll start tomorrow.'

'Yes, Mrs O'Keefe,' said Annie.

'I've been thinking about that,' said Mrs O'Keefe. 'What you're to call me, I mean. At the moment it's the name of a "horrible woman" for you, isn't it?'

'Yes,' said the children in heartfelt tones.

'I think "Auntie Connie" fits the bill don't you? I know Annie and Connie makes us sound a bit like a music hall act, but we'll get our tongues around it in time.'

The children agreed that 'Auntie Connie' sounded fine. The new auntie then went into the hall and phoned her son. They heard her say that something had come up – 'a bit of an emergency' – and that she'd be sleeping here for a bit. Could he pack her things and bring them round to Calverley Row the next day? She then lowered her voice, but misjudged it, and they heard her say: 'No, there's no danger of meeting him.'

Then she came back to the sitting room and they all watched a bit of television. 'Study and revision tomorrow,' she said, as she packed them off, earlier than of late, to bed. 'Two hours a day over the summer and you'll soon catch up.'

Annie slept wonderfully well. It was the sleep of utter relief, at a burden having been lifted off her shoulders. The future was unclear, but somehow, she knew, they were going to remain a family.

Matthew's sleep was more troubled. In fact, it was a long time before sleep came at all. He heard the lights being switched off downstairs and the house settling into total silence, and still he lay staring into the darkness. He was troubled by what Mrs O'Keefe – what Auntie Connie – had said about his father needing medical attention and not getting it, troubled about her comment that in judging him so harshly he was playing God. It was true that before . . . all this he hadn't been a bad father at all – easy-going, generous, and a lot of fun. There had always been laughter when he had been around. And yet for that one lapse he had been willing to condemn him utterly, cast him off his pedestal, break up the image. Why had he been so unforgiving?

And the accusation of playing God made him think of Carmen O'Keefe, and burying her body. Had he played God there, too? Was that another mistake they were going to have to undo?

No! he told himself fiercely. That woman was going to stay buried. Better for all of them so – for the children, for Dad, for Auntie Connie, for Rob O'Keefe.

After midnight he dropped off to sleep, and when he awoke it was to a household of which he was no longer in charge.

CHAPTER 11

Back to Normal

Matthew awoke to the smell of frying bacon. His nostrils almost twitched under the sheets at the delicious unexpectedness of it. When he went out on to the landing he found Annie and Jamie in the bathroom and the two elder ones exchanged the sort of looks that their recent complicity had made so frequent: looks that did not need words added to them. This one said all sorts of things like, 'Just like old times' and, 'We're not having to do it ourselves' and, 'We're free at last.' It was Greg who ran downstairs shouting, 'Fried breakfast! Yippee!' but he put all their feelings into those simple words.

'Now, you're not to think you'll be getting this every morning,' said Mrs O'Keefe, as she took warmed plates from under the grill and began dishing out. 'I know as well as anyone that wouldn't be good for you. But on Sundays . . .'

They all pulled back chairs and sat at table, looking at her raptly.

'We've just been having cereals and toast,' said Annie, making an advance towards friendship and intimacy – an intimacy that involved complicity as well. 'But this is wonderful. Mum used to cook us a proper breakfast at weekends.'

Annie suddenly caught sight of little Jamie, looking at Mrs O'Keefe with his brow wrinkled and she knew with certainty that he was about to ask, 'Who are you?' She jumped in quickly with, 'Now, Jamie, you'll just have to wait till Auntie Connie has done yours.'

There was a pause for thought, and then: 'Auntie Connie,' repeated Jamie, as if this solved his problem.

'That's right,' said Mrs O'Keefe, turning round and smiling. 'We talked it over last night, what you should call me, and that's what we decided on. Auntie Connie.'

'Auntie Connie,' said the two younger ones.

'You can tell people I'm a friend of your Auntie Maureen's, and I'm here to look after you till your dad is all right.'

This was a new idea to Greg.

'Is Daddy going to get well?' he asked.

'Well, we'll surely hope so, won't we? Sick people usually do get well, don't they?' She turned and began putting the plates before them. 'I'm going to make a start today by arranging for his doctor to come round.'

They all took up knives and forks and began tucking in joyously.

'His doctor's in a group,' said Matthew, his mouth full. 'I think they only have emergency calls on Sundays.'

'Does the doctor go to St Joseph's?'

'Oh yes. It's Dr Maclennan.'

'Then I'll ring him up before he goes off to Mass. If I can't speak to him, I'll speak to his wife. I'm sure she'll understand how important this is.'

Breakfast was wonderful, with unlimited toast and marmalade, though Auntie Connie said she didn't like that awful sliced stuff, and she'd have to look around for some real bread somewhere. She managed not to make it sound like a criticism. When they were finally replete, Annie and Matthew said they'd wash up, and after a moment's thought Auntie Connie nodded agreement. She went into the hall and consulted a telephone directory, and after they'd finished running the water for the washing up, the children heard fragments of conversation.

'No, there's no question of his coming to the surgery. Even if I could get him there it would just make a spectacle of the man . . . I'd say it was some kind of mental breakdown . . . No, very serious . . . Well, the children have been looking after him, bless their hearts. But now I'm here, and I'll not be going home till he's back to health . . .'

Once again Annie and Matthew looked at each other. Then they went on with the washing up. When Auntie Connie came back to the kitchen she looked very pleased.

'He'll be coming round tomorrow afternoon. That's the first step taken, isn't it? Now, I don't suppose you children have been going much to church, have you?'

They both shook their heads solemnly.

'Not much,' said Annie. 'We have been, but not much.'

'Afraid people would ask a lot of questions, were you? Well, we'll have to get you all back to regular churchgoing, but perhaps we'd better let things settle down for a week or so first. Then you can answer all people's questions confidently. And I can't go today, at least not this morning, because my Rob will be coming round with my things. So I think you two should get down to your school work, and start revising all you've done, or should have done, since your poor mother died. Don't say you haven't fallen behind, because I know you must have. It'll be six months' work, and if you give it a couple of hours every day over the summer you should be up to date by the end of the holidays.'

It was comforting to be told what to do. Perhaps it wouldn't be so pleasant for ever, because Auntie Connie obviously had very definite ideas, and rather old-fashioned ones. But for the moment it was a good feeling, and every time she told them what to do, they realized that now they didn't have to make all their own decisions, or decisions about Greg and Jamie.

Rob O'Keefe came round at about eleven o'clock. He had a long conversation with his mother in the kitchen, and then he was led through to be introduced to them, bringing with him a wonderful aroma of roasting pork. He was a big, strong-boned man with large hands and a protruding chin. He had lost his Irish accent and spoke very much as their father did, when he spoke at all. He looked to be in his early thirties, but his fair hair was already thinning. He was very ill-at-ease, and when he'd said he had seen them sometimes at church with their mother, he shuffled and didn't seem to know what else to say.

'I hear you've been going through a rough patch,' was the best he could finally manage.

'Oh, not so bad really,' said Matthew.

'I'm really sorry about your dad . . . You'll be all right now Mother's taken you in hand.'

'Yes, we will.'

Auntie Connie then took him out to meet the young ones who were playing in the back garden. When Matthew and Annie went to the kitchen for a Coke half an hour later, they saw him playing uproarious games with them, lifting Jamie high above his head and then swooping him down towards the ground as if he were a bird seizing a worm.

'He's embarrassed with us because we know about his wife and our dad,' said Annie, when they were back in the front room.

Matthew nodded wisely.

'Yes. He's what they used to call a cuckold.'

'I expect he'll get over it,' said Annie.

But it would clearly take time. Later, towards one, when his mother asked him to stay for Sunday dinner he began shuffling again and declined.

'But there's plenty for all,' Auntie Connie said. 'Annie bought in a lovely big joint.'

'We were going to have it cold on Monday,' said Annie. 'But we'd be happy if you stayed. There's some sausages we can have tomorrow.'

'No, I'll not stop. There's a lot needs doing at home before I go back on the rigs. Goodbye for now.'

And he shot off.

After dinner, the young ones went outside again, and the other three could talk. It was necessary to decide how to organize the house, and who was to sleep where.

'It's a mercy it's a good, big house, with four bedrooms,' said Mrs O'Keefe.

'Aunt Lucy inherited it from her parents,' said Matthew, who remembered her best. 'Dad was her nearest relative, and she and Mum were very close.'

'It's a blessing your dad's settled himself in the smallest bedroom too.'

'He wouldn't go into the big one, not after Mum's death.'

'Is that right? It would be upsetting, of course. Well, what if I have the big one, and Jamie's little bed in there with me? Then Matthew and Gregory can have the second, and Annie the third.' Matthew opened his mouth to protest, but she said: 'A growing girl of Annie's age needs a room to herself. I'd stay downstairs, only there really has to be a quiet room where you can both do your homework. We'll try and wean the young ones from too much television, but there's no way we can stop them making a bit of noise.'

Matthew and Annie thought it over, and then nodded. The arrangement was the best they could come to in the circumstances. Mrs O'Keefe stood up.

'I'll fetch your father's tray. I'm trying to get him used to me before the doctor comes tomorrow.'

The doctor's visit was something of a nightmare to Matthew. When they talked it over, in 1993, he said to Annie, sitting in the big armchair he had gradually grown into as the man of the house: 'I didn't take in a thing at school that day. I was sure I was going to be blamed. I was sure he was going to say Dad was like that because we didn't get help for him.'

'Even if he'd thought that, he'd never have said it,' said Annie. 'He's a kind man, is Dr Maclennan. He's always been good to us. Like coming this morning without being called in. There's not many doctors make home calls at all these days unless they're on call for emergencies.'

'He has a lot of respect for Auntie Connie.'

'Of course he does. Everybody does.'

'You don't think it's true, now, do you?'

'About Dad? No, I think Dad had been going quietly mad over the last few months of Mum's life. If anyone drove him mad it was Carmen O'Keefe.'

'I hope you're right. It's . . . not something that it's easy to live with.'

Annie was going to say something soothing, but at that moment Jamie put his head round the door and said he was going to make a pot of tea, and because they both felt they'd rather lost touch with him in the last few years, they went out to the kitchen to help him. He went about putting the kettle on and fetching cups and saucers from the cupboard with the grace of a natural, but not fanatical, athlete. Jamie, they all believed, was going to get somewhere in life. He was also very lovable, because he cared so much for other people, and was particularly protective of Auntie Connie. He had just taken a lot of good GCSEs, and was the school sprint and hurdling champion. Annie felt that they could at least have a small part of the credit for his turning out so well.

That day, in the summer of '79, Matthew came back from school with trepidation in his heart. He hoped that the doctor had been and gone, but he found Auntie Connie waiting anxiously in the kitchen, standing against the sink, unable to settle.

'I took him up there and introduced him,' she said, 'though for all the response I got I could have saved my breath. Then I left them to it. He'll not learn anything awkward from your poor Da'.'

Matthew's instinct was to make himself scarce when Dr Maclennan came down, but he forced himself to face things through.

'Well, I'm no psychiatrist,' the doctor said, 'but he looks pretty far gone to me. I can get nothing to the purpose out of him. How long has he been like this?'

'It started some time after Mum's death,' said Matthew – a prepared formula he was rather proud of.

Dr Maclennan frowned.

'That was – when? – January, wasn't it? My wife was at the funeral, and she said your father looked pretty cut up.'

'Dad always hated funerals. After that he started . . . sort of sliding down. Some days he was better, some worse, and it was difficult to put your finger on anything and say, "Now we really have to do something."'

'I see . . . Well, I'm very glad that someone has called me in now. Which doesn't make it any easier to decide what to do. Of course, I'll have to get him to a psychiatrist. Will he go willingly, do you think?'

'I don't think so,' said Mrs O'Keefe. 'I tried to get him into the fresh air this morning – just take a walk in the garden.

It can't be healthy shut up there twenty-four hours a day. But there was no way I could get him outside. The man seemed almost frightened.'

'I suppose that's understandable if he's been in there a fair while. I think I can get a psychiatrist to come here to him, if I stress the seriousness and urgency of the case. But if he says he needs to be committed, then committed he'll have to be . . . You say you'll be here to take care of the children, Mrs O'Keefe?'

'Oh yes, for as long as needs be.'

'Right, then we'll take it from there. I suppose it would be better for them if their father was out of the house?'

'No, it wouldn't,' said Matthew sturdily. 'We're quite used to him being up there. He's our father.'

It was, for Matthew, a sort of reconciliation, and absolution for Dermot.

'What do you feel?' the doctor asked Mrs O'Keefe.

'Oh, he's no problem as far as I'm concerned. The only question is what's best for him.'

'Well, I'll pass that on to the psychiatrist. But it's quite possible he'll want to take him into an institution, at least for a while.'

When he had gone, Matthew felt glad he had spoken up for his father, and for his right to stay in his own home. It seemed as if it restored a balance, righted a wrong, especially as the house would undoubtedly have been more relaxed and comfortable without his presence there. When Annie got back from school, she agreed that to have had their father shunted off to an institution would have been a hateful thing to do.

Inevitably, the fact of Dermot Heenan's condition started to get around the Catholic community, or the St Joseph's part of it. Matthew and Annie discovered that Auntie Connie had been right and Greg had already let drop some hints about his state, though his teachers had been slow to pick them up. Now, the fact that he was in need of psychiatric help spread fast, among people who were distrustful of psychiatrists and a little scared of madness. Matthew and Annie got used to looks of sympathy. One day, later in the week of the doctor's visit, Peter Leary watched for Matthew from the window of Mr Patel's supermarket and signed himself off from policing duty as he approached.

'I hear your dad's had a nervous breakdown,' he said.

It wasn't the subtlest of approaches, but Matthew didn't take it amiss because he regarded Peter as a person of goodwill.

'That's right.'

'People are saying he's been like that for months – pretty much since your mum died.'

'Well, yes, he has.'

'And you've been covering up for him all this time?'

'Sort of.'

'Wow! That must have taken some doing.'

Matthew looked down at the pavement modestly.

'We weren't exactly covering up. We were afraid of being taken into care and split up.'

'But it was brilliant never to let slip anything . . . Have you heard where she is?'

'Where who is?'

'Carmen O'Keefe, you berk!'

Matthew tried, vainly of course, to suppress a blush. The question had caught him off-guard, because he knew very well where Carmen O'Keefe was. Luckily, Peter Leary's eyes were on some lad playing with a football on the grass verge some way ahead.

'No, I don't know any more than anyone else.'

'She's her mother-in-law isn't she, the woman who's looking after you all?'

'Yes. She doesn't know anything, though. But she doesn't think she's in Leeds anywhere.'

'Why not?'

'Because Carmen is an outdoor person, always out and around, not sticking at home tied to the kitchen sink. Mrs O'Keefe thinks someone would have seen her.'

'I suppose that makes sense . . . Has she told you what happened on the day she disappeared?'

'No, I haven't even asked.'

'It'd be worth knowing if there was a big row, and what it was about.'

'I suppose so . . . But it's not an easy subject to bring up, not with Dad upstairs.'

'Does she not want to talk about her?'

'Oh, she'll talk about her. Says she was a woman with no morals, that kind of thing, and that everyone's better off without her, especially her Rob. But I don't think she'd be happy if I started asking questions.'

'Maybe not.'

'Like I was blaming her or suspecting her or something.'

'I suppose we should all just be glad that she's gone . . .' The boy thought. 'That's a point, isn't it? You say she might get the idea you suspected her. She just might have been done in, mightn't she? A woman like that . . .'

Matthew's heart thumped.

'The police don't think so. They went to the police as soon as she went missing.'

'And they think she's just run off with a man?'

'Yes.' Matthew collected his thoughts. 'You say "a woman like that", but a woman like that's more likely to run off with someone than get herself murdered.'

'I suppose so. My turning. Keep in touch.'

And with a raise of the hand he went off. Matthew went on, troubled. For the first time, the question of murder had been raised. He thought he'd coped with it all right, but it was there, now, between them.

And there was another thing. He had resolved, whenever the subject of Carmen O'Keefe came up, to talk of her in the present tense. Yet somehow he always made the odd slip into the past tense. Usually it could be justified — as speaking of someone who used to be among them but was no longer. But what if, sometime, he used the past tense about her and it couldn't be justified in that way? He wished he could transform the memories of that dreadful night when they'd buried her into nothing worse than a bad dream, and think of her as everyone else did, flaunting a new fur coat or diamonds on the arm of a rich new fancy man in Birmingham, Glasgow or Manchester.

The problem was that the more questions he asked about her, the more the possibility of murder insinuated itself into people's minds.

CHAPTER 12

The One Who Got Away

The psychiatrist didn't come till nearly a fortnight later, when the children were in their last week of school. Mrs O'Keefe had very much hoped that he would come when they were not in the house, and her wish was granted. He first talked the case over with her for a few minutes, and she retailed the slightly sanitized version which she had previously served up for Dr Maclennan. This emphasized – indeed, misrepresented – the slowness of Dermot Heenan's descent to the state he was now in, as a way of explaining the children's slowness of action. The man – in his forties, a slovenly dresser with tired eyes and a little beard – listened, nodded noncommittally, then let her take him upstairs. When he saw Dermot he turned and gave Auntie Connie a nod of dismissal, so she was forced to go down and wait for him in the kitchen.

He was up there for three quarters of an hour, and Auntie Connie was at a loss what he could be getting out of the poor soul he was dealing with in all that time. She had never had more than barely comprehensible mumblings of self-accusation from him. When the psychiatrist finally came down, he used a lot of long terms she had never met with before and then tried hard to put them simply for her. He said he thought the children must have exaggerated the slowness of the man's illness gaining the upper hand. She was glad, though, that he didn't say this in any accusing way.

'I expect it frightened them,' he said, 'and they didn't want to face up to it. They were alone here with him, you said?'

'They were, I'm sad to say. Everyone thought he was all right – a fine, healthy, straightforward soul that he was!'

'I've seen all too many healthy and straightforward people in states even worse than his,' commented the psychiatrist.

'Sure you must see many a sad sight,' said Mrs O'Keefe, a phrase she often used with doctors and nurses, and none the less sincerely meant for that.

The rest of what he said was told, suitably censored, to the older children when they came home.

'He says he needs to have him into a . . . psychiatric clinic for a few weeks, maybe a month, to do a number of tests and try a few treatments,' she said, in her comfortable, Irish countrywoman's voice. 'I've emphasized that his home is here, and he'll always be properly cared for in his own place, as long as that's what's best for him and what he wants. The psychiatrist says we're to prepare him for the move and for the treatment, though how we're to do *that* the good Lord only knows.'

What she had omitted from her account was the psychiatrist's regrets that he had not been called earlier, his feelings that it might now be too late to help the man upstairs. Matthew and Annie therefore felt fairly hopeful, and when they took food to the bedroom, or helped to wash their father and keep him generally presentable, they kept saying encouraging things about getting help for him, and about his going somewhere for treatment that would make him right again.

'Don't send me away!' was one of the things they distinguished in his mumbled protests. 'Matthew, Annie, don't send me away from my little place here!'

'Don't you want to be well again, Dad?' they said urgently, but could see no sign that he did.

When the day came for his going away, Auntie Connie decided the best thing to do was to get the children out of the house entirely. It was a fine day in late July and school had broken up. She gave Matthew and Annie five pounds and told them to take Greg and Jamie off to Roundhay Park for the day.

'We want to spare them any distress, don't we?' she said, though she didn't deceive them, and they realized that it was they too who were being spared.

When they got back, their father was gone, and the little bedroom had been aired and spring-cleaned, though Auntie Connie said it should be kept exactly as it had been so that he would feel at home when he came back. That meant keeping there Gregory's discarded Postman Pat books, and the posters for *The Railway Children* and *Mary Poppins*. Matthew realized that Auntie Connie, for one, didn't expect him to come back cured.

Dermot's going meant a very relaxed summer holiday for the children. It was almost like their last days as a real family, when their father had been away most of the time and their mother was there as a stable centre. Auntie Connie filled that role very well, and it was clear that by the end of the holidays she would be completely accepted. Annie in particular came to love and cling to her; accepting her views, following her rules, referring to her all her perplexities. Matthew accepted her presence gratefully, but kept his innermost feelings shut up, and warned Annie against confiding in her totally.

'*That* we've got to keep secret – always,' he insisted.

Both the elder children accepted that there was a lot of school work to catch up on. One of the things that would have troubled them if they had had time to think about it during their time as masters of the house was the way they had gradually fallen behind their classmates at school. Matthew in particular was ambitious, though as yet in an unspecified direction, feeling he wanted to 'make something of his life' – as his father, even before his madness, so obviously hadn't done. Since he was undecided what that 'something' would be, he felt the need to learn as much as possible on as many subjects as possible. Annie fell behind because she had other, more important goals to aim at, but she was a child who valued the approval of her elders, and when the chance came to catch up with her fellows, she seized it. The two hours a day were largely pleasurable, never merely a fag, and for the rest of the time they played hard, recognizing that this could be a last late flowering of childhood, the sweeter for being unexpected.

They still, of course, did things around the house, as all

elder children in big families do, as well as shopping and errands. Mrs O'Keefe wondered sometimes at the time it took them to shop at the supermarket, until she realized that they walked to it along the ring road instead of going across the field. When she asked them why, Annie said she didn't much like sheep – she knew it was silly, but that was the reason. Mrs O'Keefe accepted their help and often listened to their opinions. She recognized that these were children who had of necessity grown up fast, had shouldered burdens long before they should have had to. She did not fence them round with too many of the unnecessary restrictions of childhood.

'Heavens above!' she exclaimed one evening when she was doing the ironing in the kitchen and the iron exploded in a dangerous-looking blue flash. 'Haven't I been saying this auld thing was going to give up the ghost?'

'Are you hurt?' asked Annie anxiously, and she and Matthew ran over to see she was all right. She said that she'd had nothing worse than a bad turn.

'Mother used to say it was about to go,' said Annie.

'It can probably be mended,' said Matthew. 'I think it's mainly the cord. We oughtn't to buy a new one unless we have to, because I think the washing machine's about to conk out.'

'Will you let me worry about things like that now?' said Auntie Connie with humorous resignation. 'I've a bit of money of my own, and we're not going to want.'

'You shouldn't have to use your own money. And we might as well get it repaired if we can,' said Matthew, with childish persistence. 'There's a man in Bramley Town Street Dad and Mum used to take things to.'

'You can take it to him tomorrow if you've a mind to,' said Auntie Connie. 'There may be a year or two of life in it yet. That's an end to ironing for tonight, but it was almost finished anyway.'

Later that night, while Auntie Connie was boiling milk for their bedtime drink, Matthew and Annie talked over what they would do next day.

'I'm going to take it to Andy Patterson's,' Matthew said.

'Oh?'

'You can come,' he said solemnly, 'but I don't think you should come *in*. I don't think he'd talk about *her* with a girl present.'

'I don't think he'll talk about his love-life with a fourteen-year-old boy, anyway,' said Annie, stung into dismissiveness. 'What are you going to say to him? "I hear you slept with Carmen O'Keefe, just like our dad did"? I think you should let it drop. It's in the past.'

'I have let it drop . . . Only this is an opportunity.'

'An opportunity to what?'

'To . . . well, to find out how she came to be killed.'

'I don't want to know. And what good would it do, us knowing? You can go on your own.'

So next morning Matthew shoved the iron into an old leather bag and took the canal path to Bramley. Walking gave him time to think, though the problem that Annie had alluded to – that of ever getting around to the subject he wanted to talk about – was a ticklish one, and he hadn't solved it by the time he left the towpath and went up the hill towards Bramley Town Street. He had no idea where Andy Patterson's shop was, but he found it soon after he turned in off Broad Lane. The centre of Bramley had been ruined some years before by Town Hall vandals, who had pulled down the old stone houses and shops and built a hideous shopping centre and dreary council flats in their place. Patterson's Electrical Store was in one of the few old buildings remaining, and its title was more ambitious than the reality. It was a second-hand and repair shop presenting a motley array of appliances and implements up for sale or in for repair. All the surfaces – floor, counter, workbench – presented a great jumble of wires, parts, batteries and valves. Matthew did not know it, but shops of this kind were doomed, as people found they preferred to chuck away and start again rather than repair what had gone wrong.

If Andy Patterson realized this he was keeping very cheerful about it. When Matthew had pushed open the door and made a path for himself through the debris up to the counter he found a little gnome of a man, bald-headed, glinting of eye, sitting contentedly on the other side with the entrails of an ancient vacuum cleaner around him. If Matthew had been privy to Bramley gossip, he would have known that women preferred not to go into Patterson's Electrical Store on their own. As it was, he registered almost subconsciously that Andy Patterson did not seem to conform to the usual pattern of Carmen O'Keefe's boyfriends.

'And what can I do for you?' the man asked, with a friendly smile. Matthew rummaged in his bag.

'This iron – it sort of exploded last night.'

'Oh aye, I can see that.' He examined it with an undoubtedly expert eye, squinting through thick spectacles. 'Looks as if it's just the cord, but we should maybe have a look at its insides to see everything's safe. Dangerous things sometimes, are irons. Will you come back for it?'

'Could you possibly do it now? You see, I come from Rodley and I have to make the trip specially.'

'I could probably do that for you. I've only this old Hoover to puzzle my brains with. Sit you down.'

Matthew sat down on an old upright chair, considerately put there for waiting customers. The sparky little man began setting the Hoover pieces methodically around him on the floor, and Matthew could see that he was not only small but running to fat. He was just racking his brains how to start the conversational ball rolling, when Andy Patterson began it for him.

'Well now, young man, you say you're not from round here?'

'No, I'm from Rodley. I walked along the canal.'

'Not often I get folks making the pilgrimage here all the way from Rodley!'

'They said you were good with old things.'

'Did they now?' Glint went the sharp little eyes. 'Well, I'm always nice to pensioners, that's true, but I prefer a younger bit of skirt, if I can get it.' He gave a tinkling little laugh at his own joke. 'And how do you like to pass your time, young fellow?'

Matthew considered.

'Oh, I like a bit of football. I'm not so keen on cricket . . . And I like the girls too.'

It was just the right response. It was obviously the man's favourite subject. His face lit up.

'At your age, young man? Though now I come to remember, I was pretty interested myself when I was no older than you . . . Oh, those were the days.' He gazed ahead for a moment. 'There was more mystery then. How do you get that delicious sense of discovery if there's no mystery?'

'Is there a Mrs Patterson?' asked Matthew.

'There's one or two.' Andy Patterson shot a sly glance in Matthew's direction to see how he took this, then he grinned. 'Oh, women are my downfall, no question of that. No – I tell a lie: not women, but *wives*.'

'Haven't you . . . stayed married, then?'

'Not on your life. The mistake was to get married, and it would have been a greater one to stay married! Either they've walked out on me or I've walked out on them.'

'I thought you were a Catholic.'

'Now who would have told you that?' he asked, genuinely surprised. 'Oh, I was once, true enough. Brought up in the faith. But I don't think the Catholic faith is the right one for a happy-go-lucky chap like myself. It finds too many things that you need to struggle against. In the end, you give up the struggle and say, "What the hell – I'm going to do what I enjoy doing, whatever the Fathers say." Doing what I fancy has given me a lot of fun, a lot of pleasure – and a few scrapes and bloody noses too, but that's life, isn't it?'

'Doesn't it get . . . sort of dangerous, having lots of women? I mean, with husbands and that? And don't they get jealous of each other?'

'It can happen, young fellow – take it from me who knows!' He talked freely while his stubby finger poked around inside the iron. 'The thing is to keep it all nice and free and easy. You're just in it for the fun, and she's just in it for the fun. She's not your exclusive property, and you're not her exclusive property. And you neither of you are going to get plagued by fits of guilt because you neither of you think it's anything to feel guilty about. Ah, young man, you find a woman like that and you find a treasure!'

'Did you ever find one like it?'

'I did, young fellow, I did.'

'And have you still . . . got her? I mean, are you still going with her?'

The little man scratched his bald head, while the other hand fetched from under the counter a new length of lead.

'No, to tell you the truth, I'm not. They say she's gone off with a rich admirer, but I wouldn't know the truth about that.'

'Didn't she tell you about him?'

'No, she didn't. But we were finished well before that . . . Now I come to think about it, I'm contradicting my own advice when I tell you about her. Because the truth is, I had to break with her – had no choice, not if I was to sleep easy of a night. I'm a pretty happy-go-lucky fellow, like I said, but I have my rules in life, and they may not be the Fathers' rules, but they're what I live by. I wouldn't do down a friend, and I wouldn't cheat a customer, though I might cheat the taxman if I knew a good way to do it . . . that kind of rule's what I'm talking about . . .'

Matthew knew better than to interrupt, and in a moment he started up again.

'And I found that she hadn't got any rules – not just in the matter of having a bit o' fun, but not *any* rules. It was . . . unnerving, in a way. Not like anything I'd ever known . . . And when she started hinting, pretending at first it was all a joke, about something she wanted me to do – not to do when we were having fun, I don't mean that, but . . . something else – and when it became less of a joke, then I got out.'

'Dropped her?'

'Aye. We never had words, but I just didn't call her any more. She got the message, I think, because she never called me. I just brought it to an end – sharpish!'

'What –?' began Matthew. The man snapped the base of the iron over the works and began screwing it vigorously.

'No more questions, young fellow! The less anyone knows

about that the better! Now, tell your mother that with the new lead I've put on, and the tinkering I've done with the works she'll have an iron that will go for another three or four years. That will be two pounds, young fellow, and a lot cheaper than a new one, eh? You never told me your name, by the way.'

'Michael Potter,' said Matthew quickly.

'Michael Potter from Rodley. Well, come back, young man, if you ever have anything else that's broken. Next time we'll talk about you.'

Matthew escaped from the ramshackle little shop, and began the long walk with his burden. Many years later he said to Annie: 'That was the day I began to understand.'

CHAPTER 13

Rob and his Women

Matthew had plenty of time to nourish his suspicions during the rest of the school holidays, but little chance to find out more about what had been going on in those months of his mother's last pregnancy. For a while he brooded, getting nowhere. The fact that it was holiday time meant that he was unable to consolidate his acquaintanceship with Peter Leary. They were not of an age, so going to see him at his home was out. After a week, he snapped out of his mood. With the elasticity of youth he threw himself into his usual leisure pursuits, playing casual football with boys in the neighbourhood, bicycling to the woods at Calverley, organizing picnics. Auntie Connie had registered his mood, and felt it wisest to let him cope with it as best he could. She registered, too, when he came out of it, and was glad.

The end of the holidays in September would coincide with the return of their father from the institution where he had been undergoing treatment. Matthew and Annie gathered that the psychiatrist had had one or two conversations with Auntie Connie, in which he had described himself as unhopeful. He said he would do his best to call after Dermot's return and explain to them more fully what the man's mental state was, and what they could do about it. Meanwhile, the family, though unconsciously, rejoiced in his absence and had Auntie Connie's undivided attention, because Rob was back on the rigs. 'And it's not as though he needs his old mother,' she said, 'or would pay any attention to what she told him. A grown man thinks he should go his own way and make his own mistakes.'

Rob turned up again at the beginning of September, a few days before their father was due back. Auntie Connie hadn't quite known when to expect him, because, as she said, he was 'no great letter-writer,' so it was as much of a surprise to her as to the rest when he turned up on the back doorstep. What was more of a surprise still was that he had a woman with him.

'This is Grace, Ma,' he said, with a touch of bravado to mask embarrassment. 'A friend.'

Matthew noticed a quick tightening of Auntie Connie's lips, before she stood aside.

'Come in, Grace,' she said.

They all crowded into the kitchen, and there introductions were made. Grace seemed to find it easy to remember which of the children was which, so perhaps she had been coached a little in advance. But it was much too crowded in there, so the younger ones were sent out to play and the older ones went through to the living room, where Auntie Connie busied herself clearing the armchairs and the sofa of children's books and toys, and then set Annie on to making tea for them all.

'Isn't it nice here?' said Grace at the window. 'It's a lovely house, and then you've got country right on your doorstep. It's not how I imagined Leeds at all.'

'We think it's nice,' said Matthew.

So, Grace, apparently, was new to Leeds. Matthew and Annie both liked her right from the start. She was quite a short person, especially beside Rob, but she was plump and vivacious – positively bubbling when the subject matter was kept light. Her mouth was small, but curved upwards in a rosebud bow, as if she was perpetually amused by life and her part in it. She had no particular clothes sense, but no need of it either: her presence was in her body and her smile, and both were inviting. There was no tightness about her body; no calculation in her mind. A greater contrast with Carmen O'Keefe could hardly be imagined.

'I liked Grace right from the start,' Annie said in 1993, when she and Matthew and Jamie were chattering over tea and biscuits in the kitchen, waiting for Greg to arrive from the north-east.

'So did I,' said Matthew. 'And she's been the making of Rob.'

'She said I could go and live there,' said Jamie.

Annie looked at him with something like jealousy in her face.

'You're coming to us,' she said firmly. 'Ted and I both want to have you, and the children will be over the moon.'

Annie and her family lived in a meagre little house on a commercially-built estate, with paper-thin walls and tiny bedrooms. Yet it had never occurred to her not to offer Jamie a home. She was the only one of the family that could provide him with the proper stable background.

'Oh yes, I'm coming to you. I wouldn't want to go to university in Leeds, where I would know half of the other students already. But it was nice of her to ask, I thought. And I'd have been quite happy there.'

'She has the knack of making people happy,' said Matthew.

But back in 1979, they were just beginning the process of getting to know her.

'So you don't know Leeds, then?' asked Auntie Connie, her eyes interestedly summing her up. Annie knew then there were conflicting hopes and fears going on in her mind.

'Never been here in my life. Tell you the truth, I imagined it was all grime and heavy industry.'

'Grace is from Grimsby,' put in Rob.

'Grimsby?' said Auntie Connie. 'Is that fish?'

'Yes, Grimsby is fish.'

'So that's where you will have met, then: when Rob was on his way to the rigs?'

The two turned and smiled at each other, intimately.

'Got it in one, Ma!' said Rob, pulling his eyes away. 'I told you Ma would be curious, Grace.'

'Of course she'd be curious!' said Grace, with her ringing laugh. 'What mother isn't curious about her son's girl-friends?'

Mrs O'Keefe's mouth tightened again.

'I'm not sure I like the idea of girlfriends. Rob is still a married man, you know.'

Rob was more relaxed now, and simply laughed.

'Give it a rest, Ma! Carmen's gone off, and she won't be coming back. If she did, I'm not sure I'd have her back.'

'Well, I'm glad you've seen the light!' said Auntie Connie. 'But that's not to say you should get someone else in her place.'

'How did you meet?' asked Annie hurriedly, setting out cups and saucers round the table. Auntie Connie's religion was still a rather unpredictable factor in their lives, and she judged that a little lecture on Catholic Marriage was a possibility, for all that she had obviously disliked Carmen.

'Oh, I've known her for a time, haven't I, Grace?'

'Just to nod to and swap a joke with.'

'Grace's on the other side of the counter at this marvellous transport caff, just outside Grimsby. I always stop there on my way to the rigs. They serve the best ham and eggs I know.'

So that accounted, more or less, for Grace: she had served Rob his ham and eggs over the years. Presumably recently, or at some time, friendship had ripened, but it was difficult to ask about that without seeming to want a blow-by-blow account.

'So now you've come to have a look at Leeds, have you?' asked Auntie Connie.

'That's right,' said Grace, perfectly relaxed. 'I've been working all summer, because the others in the café have children with school holidays. So I arranged to take the weeks I was due for when Rob came off the rig.'

'I hope she's going to like Leeds,' said Rob. 'Then mebbe she'll stay.'

It was said with deceptive casualness. His mother looked concentratedly down at the teapot she was pouring from, making an effort to say nothing.

'That's a bit of a maybe still,' said Grace, 'but I'm sure I'm going to like Leeds. I do already. And I like this house, too.' She looked around the room. 'It's such a *family* place, so lived in . . . I'm sorry. I'm forgetting that you lost your mother. And your dad is – '

'Yes,' said Matthew and Annie together.

'Oh, we're getting the family together again, never fear,' said Auntie Connie. 'And a house with children in it is always going to have a nice lived-in feeling.'

That remark showed them plainly that Auntie Connie was pulled in two directions.

Rob stirred in his chair.

'There you go again, Ma! Yes, I *know* my house never had that feeling.'

'I didn't mean that, my boy! Don't take me up like that.'

'You've said it often enough before. Well, I always wanted children, but thinking about it now I wonder if it would have been a good idea. I can't see a child with Carmen as a mother having much of a chance.'

'Well, at least your eyes are open to Carmen at last,' said his mother, her mouth once again working in little twitches of disapproval. 'It used to drive me mad, the way you couldn't see.'

'I saw more than you think,' said Rob, taking a big draught of his tea. 'Being away on the rigs so much of the time, I didn't think I had the right to object. But this isn't talk for children's ears. Let's bury Carmen, shall we?' Matthew jumped, and then looked around hoping nobody had noticed. 'It's not a nice subject. And as to having children – well, it's not too late!'

Grace punched him in the ribs and laughed. And Annie noted that when he said this Auntie Connie did seem torn: she screwed up her lips, but there was something in her eyes that told Annie that she longed to have grandchildren. Auntie Connie said to Grace:

'So you've been married yourself? You've no children?'

'I've been married, but I've not had children. It was a very brief marriage. I found out in a matter of weeks it'd been a dreadful mistake.'

'So you're . . . divorced, are you?'

'Oh, yes. I'm not a Catholic, by the way.'

'I see.'

Rob shifted uneasily in his chair.

'Come off it, Ma! The world has changed. Catholics have changed. Even Catholics in Ireland have changed! I noticed that when I went back last time. The priests aren't the tyrants they once were — or if they are, most people just decide to go their own way. You've got to go with the times too. You can't stay back in the old days, when the priests and bishops told you what you could read, what you could do, and what you could think!'

It was a very long speech for him, and he sank back in his chair. His mother sighed.

'There's some things I wouldn't want to go along with. What is right and wrong doesn't change.'

Grace put on her most serious face.

'I think we should tell your mother what the position is, Rob,' she said. 'So everything's out in the open. We wouldn't be asking her to approve, just telling her, so she knows.'

'Well, you tell her, love.'

Grace turned to Mrs O'Keefe.

'Rob and I are . . . together now. I mean, while he's back on land, as a sort of trial. It happened when he was on his way to his tour of duty in July. Like I said, before we'd just swapped greetings and jokes, but when he stopped at the café in July, business was slack and I was there on my own and we really had a good talk and — well, one thing led to another, you know how it is.'

Rob put in hurriedly: 'Ma, don't look like that. Grace doesn't mean it ever happened to you, she means it's how it often happens, and you must know it does. Even in Ireland it does!'

His mother's lips remained pursed.

'Anyway,' Grace resumed, not too disconcerted, 'we don't know yet how serious it is. But I've got to say it is beginning to feel serious at the moment. We know we can't get married. For myself that doesn't matter all that much. I think before long, if we're together permanently, Rob might want to, and if Carmen turns up wanting a divorce or agreeing to one, then that might be what happens.'

'Divorce isn't p —' began Mrs O'Keefe.

'Ma, divorce is possible for *me*,' said Rob firmly.

'Anyway, there's not much point in speculating about that, is there?' said Grace, putting aside the serious mood and reverting to her normal self. 'She hasn't turned up, and she's probably perfectly happy with things as they are. And I must say, I am too. If I decide to move in with Rob permanently I'll pack in my job and look for one in Leeds. Someone who can do a good fry-up is never out of work for long. Or I might try up-market and go for a proper restaurant or hotel job.'

'So you're a good cook generally, are you?' asked Auntie Connie, feeling this was an uncontroversial subject.

'Other than fry-ups? Yes, I am. Ask Rob. And I'd quite like to try my hand at something foreign and difficult. Of course, we wouldn't want to have children until we were quite sure that things were working out.'

'Before long I'm going to have to think of a job on dry land,' said Rob. 'I'm not getting any younger.'

'If you'd got one sooner –' began Auntie Connie, but then she stopped, her thoughts written all over her face.

'Right, Ma. What you were going to say was, if you'd got one sooner, Carmen might have kept on the straight and narrow and our marriage might not have ended in disaster. And then you wondered whether it was true, and whether you'd have wanted that, even if it *was* true. The fact is, Ma, Carmen would have had other men even if I'd been home with her a hundred per cent of the time. Maybe, without realizing it, that's why I kept on with my job on the rigs. It was less painful being away than being around and unable to stop it.'

Mrs O'Keefe shook her head.

'It's wicked to say I wouldn't have wanted your marriage to succeed. It's true I knew from the start she wasn't the woman for you, but once you were married – well, of course, I'd have done anything to keep you together.'

'Maybe, Ma, maybe. We won't argue about it. Anyway, the fact is, now I've got a girl who's a million times better than Carmen, so let's forget her, shall we? Oh – before we do –'

He had begun rummaging around in his jacket.

'Yes?'

'When I got home yesterday, I found this from the insurance company.'

He had dived around in his inside pocket and produced what the children could see was a cheque. He handed it over to his mother, and when she had looked at it she raised her eyebrows.

'You can't keep this.'

'Of course I can't keep it, Ma,' said Rob disgustedly. 'It's the insurance money from her mother's death. As a matter of fact, I was tempted to send it back with: "Not known at this address" on it.'

'You couldn't just do that,' said Grace. 'Whatever Carmen is, that money's hers by right. You've got to make some effort to get it to her.'

'Couldn't you go to a lawyer and see what's best to do?' asked Mrs O'Keefe.

Rob shook his head.

'I never had any truck with lawyers, and I don't want to have.'

'I bet if you had an accident on the rig you'd go to one quick enough, to get compensation,' Grace pointed out.

'Anyway, what I thought was, I'd write to the insurance company, returning the cheque and explaining the position. I was wondering if young Matthew could help with that.'

'What, write the letter?' asked Matthew.

'Yes. I'm no great shakes at writing. And you're educated, or on the way to being . . .'

Rather unhappily, Matthew fetched a pen and sat down at the table. It seemed like a sort of lying, writing this letter, but he wanted it done and the subject of Carmen out of the way. He shut out the talk in the room and began to write.

Dear Sir, he began, *I enclose with this letter the cheque you recently sent to my wife, Carmen O'Keefe. She left me* – after a moment's thought he crossed out *me* and resumed *home in June, and since then I have heard nothing about her whereabouts.* Matthew felt that last a rather good word, and was proud of it. *If I should hear where she is, I will inform you immediately. Yours faithfully, Robert O'Keefe.*

He got up from the table and took it over to Rob.

'Now that's what I call a businesslike letter!' he said when he had read it. 'Nice to have someone in the family that can do these things.'

'But what about if she's dead?' Matthew heard himself asking. 'Wouldn't the money be yours then?'

'Nay, lad, Carmen's not dead!' said Rob with conviction, as if she'd come with a God-given certificate of immortality. 'Carmen's with a man somewhere or other. And if she was dead, I wouldn't want that money. I never liked her mother, and I had as little to do with her as I possibly could. Now, I'll copy this out in my horrible handwriting, and we can put Carmen behind us.'

So for the rest of the visit they talked about something else. True, the topic of Dermot Heenan and his mental state came up, which put most of them in mind of Carmen. But soon the younger children came in from the garden and demanded that Rob go out there and play with them. Grace went too, and they all four began a series of races and rough games that had them laughing and shouting. Auntie Connie, piling up crockery on the draining-board, looked out at the scene wistfully.

'They play beautifully, that they do,' she said.

'He's good with children, your Rob, isn't he?' said Annie.

'He is – always has been.'

'Maybe he and Grace will have some of their own.'

'But they'd be b –' She pulled herself up. 'But I'll not judge. That's not for me. It wouldn't be their fault, would it, the poor babies?'

'Why don't you go out with them?' Annie said. 'We can do the washing up.'

'Look at him with Jamie, and isn't Jamie loving it? Well, maybe I will, Annie, love. I've got to remember that you're my family now, haven't I? You're all the grandchildren I need.'

As she took off her apron and went out into the sunshine and laughter, Annie started running hot water into the basin.

They began the task without talking, but Matthew's preoccupation eventually found words.

'They really ought to know that Carmen is dead,' he said.

'Why? You heard what Rob said. He wouldn't take the money even if she was.'

'That's what he *said*,' said Matthew sceptically. 'But do you think in a year's time, if it was established that she was dead, he'd still be refusing it?'

Annie sluiced a few more saucers and then said:

'It was a big amount. Did you see Auntie Connie's face?'

'Yes. It's Rob's money by right. He feels he doesn't want it now because Carmen's gone and he's just woken up to what she was, but if it's really a huge amount he probably won't think like that for ever.'

'He might. I don't think he's a money sort of person.' She turned to look at him. 'But what if the real reason why he doesn't want it is because he killed her, and taking the money would make him feel even more guilty?'

That was a real facer. It was a full minute before Matthew could reply.

'Anyway, there's no point in discussing it. We can't tell them. If Rob did it, he wouldn't want the body found. And if they brought in the police and told them where we buried the body, the police would be bound to think we killed her in the first place.'

'You're right,' said Annie thoughtfully. 'We can't tell them. And I really don't think Rob wants that money.'

'Maybe not. Anyway, it could be that after a certain time the insurance company presumes she's dead and gives the money to – what's he called? – the next of kin or something.'

That took them into realms of legal speculation, which they could not cope with. They spent the rest of the day happily playing and talking and eating, and by the end they really felt like a happy family group. When Rob had referred to Matthew as 'family' earlier, it had felt funny, but by the end of the day it had begun to seem to Matthew and Annie as if Rob and Grace were part of their family, and that they were part of theirs.

It was only later, thinking in bed, as he often did, that

something odd occurred to Matthew. It had not occurred to him before because he knew Carmen O'Keefe was dead. But now, putting himself in the place of people who assumed she was still alive, it seemed to him that they ought to have wondered whether Carmen O'Keefe wasn't the last person on earth to disappear without trace just when she was expecting a big cheque from an insurance company. She might have been tempted away by a rich admirer, but she certainly would have made sure people knew where she was.

And yet that thought hadn't occurred to Rob, or Grace, or Auntie Connie. Was that because they weren't all that bright, or weren't thinking straight in the aftermath of Carmen's disappearance? Matthew thought that if he were a police-man, he might assume that they did not entertain that doubt either because they suspected, or because they knew, that Carmen was dead.

Talking About Carmen

Rob and Grace came round a couple of times before Dermot Heenan returned home from the mental hospital. Then their visits became more occasional for a time, with Rob patently more uneasy – unwilling to come beyond the kitchen, shuffling his feet, throwing uneasy glances ceilingwards if he thought he heard a noise upstairs. But Grace chaffed him about this, and soon he was behaving quite normally, at least in the downstairs of the house. Dermot was easy to forget.

He was brought back to Calverley Row by an attendant at the institution – a capable-looking man who was empowered by the psychiatrist to 'explain the situation'. He said that there had been a 'real improvement', but in practice this seemed to mean no more than that Dermot now had an occupation: he made rugs, and would sit happily for hours with his hook and uniform lengths of wool, filling row after row on the square of rug canvas. It obviously soothed his mind, making the outbursts of self-accusation less frequent and bitter. That was the full extent of the improvement so far as his family could see. The psychiatrist never paid the promised visit, but he had written a short note with his telephone number on it. He apparently did not envisage Dermot returning to anything like normality, but he said that his progress (or his *condition*) would be monitored: he would return to the institution on a non-residential basis every three months or so for a day of checks and tests. Effectively, this meant he was a fixture at the house in Calverley Row for the foreseeable future.

When he had been driven back, he had got out of the car

uncertainly, but once through the front door he had limped upstairs, if not like a homing pigeon, then at least like a rat scurrying back to its lair. Auntie Connie stood in the doorway shaking her head with pity. When Matthew and Annie, a minute or two later, took up a half-finished rug the attendant had handed to them, they found him looking round with child-like pleasure at the walls and furniture of his little prison. 'Good to be home, Annie, love,' he muttered, with a little whimper of pleasure. When Auntie Connie took him up a cooked meal later on he blinked at her as if uncertain whether he had seen her before or not, but in a day or two he accepted her, perhaps under the impression she was some kind of housekeeper.

The rug-making certainly seemed to help. Dermot would sit at it for hours, though he never mastered patterns, and the single-coloured rugs soon seemed to cover every room in the house. When a rug was finished, and Auntie Connie had put the finishing touches to it by sewing the edges underneath and replacing any of the knotted strands that had been clumsily done, they would take the card with wool samples up to him and with something like pleasure he would pick the colour for his next rug. Soon friends and fellow-worshippers had rugs made by Dermot, and then bazaars at St Joseph's had them as a regular feature. They became eventually a drug on the market, and were offered to charity shops and to the bazaars run by other churches. Luckily Auntie Connie had become good friends with Mrs O'Connor at the Social Security office and managed to get a grant towards the cost of the wool, on the grounds that it was occupational therapy.

'Which indeed it is,' said Auntie Connie.

With school started again, the friendship between Matthew and Peter Leary began to blossom. It was an odd school friendship, as both boys recognized. They even fabricated a reason for it, to allay the curiosity of their peers. Peter was a fanatical stamp collector, with the ambition of becoming a stamp dealer. Matthew had collected stamps for some time, but had lost interest a year or two before. Now he revived that interest, and sat at Peter's feet to learn the finer points of philately. In a short time, his interest and enthusiasm became quite genuine, but this did not alter the fact that they had been quite consciously created to form a bond between them. It enabled them to talk together in the school playground, and it accounted for Matthew's frequent visits to Peter's home. Eventually, Peter came round to Calverley Row, rather nervously at first, but eventually, like Rob, accepting the situation there as something almost normal. On one of these visits, when he slipped upstairs to the lavatory, he encountered Dermot Heenan. After that the friendship was strengthened by sympathy.

The bond lasted into their adult life. Whenever he came back to Leeds, Matthew went round to see Peter, became godfather to one of his children, helped him get another job when his stamp dealership went bust in the slump of the early 'nineties. When he and the other members of the family came back in 1993, he rang him from the house in Calverley Row. 'I think the last act is beginning,' he said. 'It's an odd feeling.'

Quite soon into the new term at school, Matthew discovered that the Holmes boy, who was now in the fifth form, was no relation to Kevin Holmes, the garage proprietor who had been named at the Irish Club as one of Carmen's lovers. So that was a possible avenue of investigation closed up. The thought of the man being a garage proprietor, though, put Matthew in mind of their own garage, and the car rusting away in it. It was frustrating being just fourteen, and having to wait so long before he could apply for a licence. One evening when Annie was having a rare night out with a friend at the ballet in Bradford, he opened up the subject with Auntie Connie.

'It's a pity about the car, just sitting there in the garage,' he said.

'It is that. But I'd feel awkward, trying to sell it.'

She was knitting peaceably, and they were both sipping their late-night Horlicks and paying very little attention to the television.

'You mean that you'd be admitting that he'll never get well again?' Matthew asked. Auntie Connie nodded.

137

'Something like that. And it's simply not mine to sell.'

'You haven't got a licence yourself?'

'I have not.'

'Didn't you ever try to learn?'

She stopped knitting, a reminiscent smile on her face.

'Well now, I did once. That was when my Pat was beginning to fail, and we both thought it might come in useful. At that time you could get a driving licence in Ireland just by paying your money – none of this nonsense about tests!'

'It's a pity you didn't buy one, then.'

'That it's not! Not for the other people on the road, it's not! Because when we went out on the road I didn't like it at all – and that was just country roads in Ireland, with hardly a thing on them except the occasional horse and cart.'

'Horses can be frightening on the road. You always think they might bolt. Maybe it was that you didn't like.'

'I didn't like the feeling of being in charge of the powerful thing. Oh, I could *do* it all right – change gears, even stop and start on a hill. I'm not a complete fool. But I got in such a state every time I sat behind the wheel that my Pat said we'd best call it a day.'

'It would be good to have the use of the car – fetching heavy things from the supermarket and that.'

'It would that,' said Auntie Connie, nodding placid agreement. 'I'll have to find someone who'll deliver us a great big sack of potatoes, then it won't be so bad. And there's a man who calls with pop at some of the houses round here. Potatoes and pop; they're the heaviest things we buy, and we buy lots of both.'

Matthew refused to be diverted.

'I can get the car out of the garage and . . . on to the road.' She looked at him. He returned the look wide-eyed. 'We could go up and down Calverley Row.'

'We'll do nothing of the kind!' said Auntie Connie determinedly. 'It would be totally illegal. If you're hinting I should get a driving licence, you can forget it. Just listening to the traffic on the ring road makes me dizzy.'

'There's another way round to the supermarket, via Calverley, though it is a lot longer.'

'You'll never get me behind that wheel, my lad, so you might as well stop trying. I suppose what it comes down to is, I'm old-fashioned, and I don't think it's ladylike.'

'Carmen drove a car.'

'There you are, then!'

Once the switch of topic was made, Matthew pursued it fairly ruthlessly.

'Was it her own car?'

'It was that. Rob bought it for her. She always called it "The second-hand Renault Rob bought me". As if she should have had a new Rolls-Royce.'

'Did she take it with her when she went away?' he asked cunningly, knowing the answer.

'She did not! I should think she was whisked off by someone in a new Rolls-Royce – or Mercedes anyway!'

'You didn't see her go?'

'Sure, I've told you I did not. If I'd seen her go, I'd have had a better idea where she might have gone. If I'd been there, I might have tried to stop her, though I don't know . . .' She shook her head, doubtingly. 'It's difficult, isn't it, when your religious faith tells you one thing, and everything in you is crying out another thing entirely. I know it's the religious faith that's right, but – well, I suppose I'm as weak as the next person. Maybe I'd have let Carmen go and said, "Good riddance". Because I knew she'd never be anything but trouble and heartache to poor Rob.'

'Was Rob away on the rigs when she took off?'

Auntie Connie shook her head.

'Oh no, he'd been back almost a week. Otherwise I wouldn't have been there, I can tell you. When I came over on a visit, Carmen was always nice as pie the first day, but even by the second day it was beginning to wear thin. So I made Rob tell me when he'd be back, and I came a day or two before, to make sure he got a proper welcome. I came every year, but just the once. Carmen wouldn't have had me in the house more often than that.'

'So Rob must have been out that night as well.'

'He was. A darts final at the Dog and Pheasant, which he'd

been looking forward to all week. So Carmen must have planned it for that night.'

'Knowing you and Rob would be out?'

'I was *got* out,' said Auntie Connie firmly. 'I don't much like pubs and darts matches and things like that. They're for men, poor weak creatures! So I'd have been in, maybe knitting and watching television and keeping myself to myself, because by then the little courtesies were getting very forced between Carmen and me. But in the morning Carmen came back from shopping – how she could shop, that woman! – and said she'd met Mary O'Hara wherever she'd been, and she'd said could I go round that evening because she was redecorating her living room and she was in a tizzy, unable to decide on a paper.'

'Is Mrs O'Hara a friend of yours?'

Auntie Connie nodded vigorously. You always knew who she approved of.

'She is that, though she's a younger woman. Comes from County Clare like myself. And she knows I like doing a bit of decorating – I'm a dab hand with the paint pot, and with the papering too. We'll get down to this place before long. But of course Carmen knew that too – cunning little minx that she is! I should have suspected.'

'Why should you have?'

'Because she was on tenterhooks all day. Just fizzling away inside, or that's what it seemed like. Couldn't settle to anything, kept making odd little remarks, snide comments and muttering little gems of nastiness that I couldn't hear and thought were probably directed at me. We'd got to that stage, you see. Rob was out most of the time, playing a round of golf with some friends – he needs his exercise when he's back off the rig. But looking back on it, I realize that Carmen had got her escape all planned out: she could hardly hide her excitement.'

'But if it was all planned out, why didn't she take her clothes and things?' Matthew asked.

'Because it was a new life – and a new life with a much richer man than my Rob, who she believed would fit her out in the sort of clothes he'd expect his woman to have,' said Auntie Connie confidently. 'And that would have suited Carmen fine.'

'So you went off to visit Mrs O'Hara?'

'That I did. About seven-thirty or so, and it's a walk of maybe half an hour. It was a nice summer evening, so I didn't take the bus. And when I got there the house was dark and there was no answer to my knocking. Well, of course, I waited around for a bit, thinking Mary'd been detained somewhere, but before long the sun went down and I walked home. And by that time the house was empty and Carmen was gone.'

'Did you think anything of it at the time?'

'Good heavens, no! I thought Carmen had gone out — probably with some man or other. I watched the ten o'clock news and then I went to bed. To tell you the truth, I didn't want to be there when she got back and have to listen to her lies. I heard Rob come in and then I went to sleep.'

'Weren't you worried in the morning?'

She pursed up her lips. Women who stayed out all night had a very definite place in her personal circles of hell.

'Well, we wondered — of course we wondered! Rob couldn't think where she'd gone. But I questioned him a bit about whether she'd ever been out for the night before when he'd been home. And he had to admit that she had — not often, but she had. I don't like to go too closely into it — whether she'd told lies, or whether she'd admitted she'd been with a man. I felt embarrassed — embarrassed with my own son! I suppose I felt sorry for him too; that he'd had to put up with his wife behaving like that, so I didn't ask too many questions. Anyway, we agreed that, Carmen being what she is, we couldn't dash straight along to the police. She might just breeze in that evening and make us look fools. It was difficult even to ring around to people to ask if they'd seen her. So we just sort of sat around, waiting for her to turn up.' Auntie Connie screwed up her face with distaste. 'It was difficult, I can tell you. Shaming.'

'How long was it before you went to the police?'

'Oh, I forget. Three days, was it? Maybe four. It was Rob who went. They took all the particulars, of course, but when they asked him about other men in her life, and when he told them what kind of woman she was, they rather lost interest. They said she must have gone off with someone, and she'd probably make contact before very long. So if we ever hear any more of Carmen, it won't be because of the police. Either we make inquiries ourselves, and I can't see the point of that, or she decides to make contact again with us.'

Matthew opened his mouth to mention the insurance money, and then closed it again. To raise the possibility of Carmen's death, and to give such solid grounds for believing in it, would be to make it clear that he himself didn't believe the accepted version of her disappearance. And that might threaten the whole basis on which the family life of the Heenans had been re-established. No, much better to keep quiet. He had already gone as far as he ought with his questions, though it was natural enough that he should be interested in Carmen and her disappearance.

'Time for your bed, young man,' said Auntie Connie. 'No reason for you to be tired out tomorrow, just because your sister goes gallivanting off to the ballet!'

Over the next few days, Matthew began rearranging the new information in his head. On the last day of her life Carmen had been on tenterhooks about something. Auntie Connie assumed that it was on account of some new man in her life who was coming that evening to sweep her away to a life of glamour and excitement. She was wrong, of course. But that left Matthew with a mystery. Presumably, whatever it was that was causing Carmen to get so worked up all day was the same thing that had brought her round to Calverley Row that evening. She had been out shopping during the day: had she heard something then, perhaps? If so, from whom? And what could it have been?

Matthew, thinking these thoughts on the way to school, frowned in concentration: something was wrong here. Auntie Connie had said she had been *shopping*. But what day had it been when she was killed? He was sure that there was school next day, because he had missed the morning through exhaustion. But earlier on the day of her death he had been working in the garden – which was how he had come to leave the carving knife on the kitchen windowsill. Surely Carmen had been killed on a *Sunday*. If so, she had probably not been shopping, but doing something else. Had that something else, whatever it was, led to her making one more attempt to find out what was going on in Calverley Row?

And then there was the question of Rob. Rob had been at a darts match. Matthew didn't know a great deal about pubs, but it seemed to him likely that if he had been *playing* in a darts match it would have been very difficult for him to disappear for a while, whereas if he had merely been *watching* it . . .

The next weekend, on a sunny Saturday, Matthew dived into the cupboard under the stairs, rummaged around, and emerged with an old dartboard and a set of darts. He had sometimes played with his father in the past, though Annie had never liked the game and kept the younger children well away. So now he played on his own, in a rather desultory fashion, until he heard Rob and Grace at the back door, paying a regular visit. Then he began playing Round the Clock with more enthusiasm.

'That's a lovely game,' said Rob, coming out before long. 'Keep at it and you'll be a champion.'

'Beat you at Round the Clock,' said Matthew, handing him the darts.

'Oh, I'm a dreadful player. I haven't got the eyesight. But it's a fine game to watch.'

When Rob was still on seven, while Matthew had gone all round the clock, there was little doubt in the boy's mind that Rob had merely been watching a darts game on the night that Carmen died.

CHAPTER 15

The Learys

'Dad's a lot worse,' said Jamie, pushing back a stray lock from his nearly-grown-up face. 'A whole lot worse.'

'So you said in your letter,' said Annie, her face concerned over the big pot of tea they had brewed. 'I would have come to help if I could. What sort of worse?'

'It started – oh – a couple of months ago, just when Auntie Connie got sick. Maybe the two are connected. I suppose in a way she jollied him along, kept him up to the mark. First of all he gave up his rug-making.'

'There will be rejoicing in Wilton, and Allah will be praised throughout the realms of Persia,' said Matthew.

They all laughed. Laughing when the subject of their father came up had been a familiar form of release for them for many years now. They sometimes felt guilty about it, but how could they feel love or loyalty for someone who had never meant a great deal in their lives, and was now nothing but a millstone?

'We were throwing them away by the end,' said Jamie. 'It was funny: it was as if he couldn't physically manage it any more, and didn't care either. It didn't distress him: he just seemed to slip further and further back – regress, that's the word, isn't it? Then he couldn't seem to take care of himself, even to the extent he used to.'

'By the time I left home he could be relied on at least to bath himself,' said Matthew. 'Except that he'd stay in forever if we'd let him.'

'That went, then I had to wash him, then – well, I won't go into the other things, they're too nasty. You'll have to go in and see him. But the fact is, he seems to have lost all control of himself, and all will to live.'

'He never had much of that,' said Annie. 'Not after Mum died. Sad that you have no memories of how he was before.'

'I'm sadder I have no memories of Mum,' said Jamie. 'But Auntie Connie's been my mother. I couldn't have had a better. Dad has just, well, always been there. A fact.' He smiled. 'You know, I think when I was young I thought it was a normal fact of life, as if everyone had one.'

'What about the social services?' asked Matthew. 'Have you been along and told them the situation?'

Jamie spread out his hands in a gesture of helplessness.

'You know how it is these days. Stretched to the limits and beyond. Local government cutbacks all round. Even Mrs O'Connor couldn't get any help for us.'

'For *you*,' said Annie. 'You've had it all to do.'

'Oh, it's only in the last few days that Auntie Connie has got really helpless . . . Mrs O'Hara has been very good, and several others from church.' He looked at his watch. 'Greg should be here soon. He said his train got in about four.'

'How is he?'

'Overworked and underpaid, if you believe him. He says selling properties in the north-east is like trying to sell ice-makers in Siberia. He had to grovel to get permission to come down. They said the deathbed of an aunt didn't warrant time off.'

'She really was a mother to you two,' said Matthew. 'Do you think we should go up and see her before Greg comes? I mean, just in case?'

'I know she wants to see us all together,' said Jamie. 'I'll nip up and see how she is – just in case, like you say.'

There was an expression of great tenderness on his face as he left the kitchen and mounted the stairs with a hurdler's litheness. When he came down, he said she was sleeping.

What impressed Matthew and Annie back in 1979 was in fact Auntie Connie's energy. She was not a young woman then, and seemed to them positively an old one, but she apparently needed very little rest or sleep. If she was watching television with them or listening to the radio in the kitchen, she was always doing something else as well – knitting, sewing, darning, peeling potatoes or slicing beans. From the moment she took over the house in Calverley Row, the routine of the household, including the tending of their father, went like clockwork.

That didn't mean that the children didn't have their own tasks and duties. That was what they were used to as older children, and that was what they would have wanted, given the choice. Auntie Connie relied on them particularly for shopping, for she never relented over the car, and it was some years before Matthew could pass his driving test – which he did, when he was eighteen, triumphantly at the first attempt. About a year after she came, pressed for time, Matthew and Annie went across the field to the supermarket. Any disturbance to the turf had long since grown over, so they had difficulty identifying where they had buried Carmen. 'Sheep aren't really so terrifying after all,' Annie said, when they got home. After that they always took the field route, and sometimes took Greg and Jamie with them – the innocent, unconscious bystanders at Carmen's death.

The beautiful regularity and efficiency of the domestic routine in Calverley Row left Matthew and Annie with quite a lot of spare time to pursue their own interests. They soon caught up with their classmates at school, so the work that Auntie Connie decreed over the summer paid off. Annie's outside interests, apart from ballet, were mainly domestic: she was already training for the housewifely role she was destined (and wanted) to fill – a role already becoming old-fashioned in the early 'eighties. She took lessons in sewing and dressmaking from Mrs Harcourt, and also helped Auntie Connie to redecorate the house. Matthew played football energetically and successfully, but he also penetrated further and further into the philatelic mysteries that fascinated Peter Leary. That meant he could spend quite a lot of time in the Leary household.

On the surface, it was a household not unlike his own before the death of their mother. After Peter came Sally, the girl in Annie's year at school, and after her came Martin, a lively boy of nine.

'When I found out what was making them come,' said their father, on one of his rare appearances when Matthew was around, 'I made sure I stopped it.' And he added rather pugnaciously: 'Priests or no bloody priests.'

Matthew thought that rather an unpleasant thing to say when his children were around, calculated to make them feel unwanted. His mother had always been careful what she said when pregnant, though the older children had known that the last pregnancy was unplanned and unwanted, as well as medically inadvisable. The remark was typical of Jim Leary, however. He made no effort to be loved.

But mostly Jim was an absent force in the household, being either on duty at the fire station or sleeping when he had been on night shift. Then the house was unnaturally quiet, all the children being old enough to honour the house rules.

'Dad's got a heavy hand,' said Peter, which again shocked Matthew. He had to admit that his dad, with all his faults and inadequacies, had never struck any of his children.

Mrs Leary was a dumpy body, someone whose attractions had long faded, and whose life was now centred on bringing up her family; feeding and clothing them on a smallish income, setting them a good example and keeping them on the straight and narrow. In this, she was not unlike Ellen Heenan, and she was similarly successful. Matthew took to the family at once, and saluted it as a nice, normal unit; one he could fit into without any feeling of strangeness. Beneath her comfortable exterior, Bridget Leary had a steely backbone: if she said a thing was to be done, it was done; if she said something was out of the question, the matter was never raised again. Matthew not only recognized the pattern from his own life; he knew instinctively that it was a pattern that could be replicated in millions of working-class homes over the centuries: the mother as ruler, arbiter and moral centre of family life. It was a pattern which Annie, when she married in 1987, began unconsciously repeating.

In such a unit, the father can come to seem something of

an intrusion. Ellen Heenan had never allowed that to happen in her family, helped by the bluff good nature of her husband. When he was home, there was usually laughter and uproarious physical games. Matthew thought that would probably be how it was with Rob and Grace, if they were ever to have a family. But in the Leary family, Jim was unquestionably some kind of outsider. Matthew wondered whether this was because he seemed seldom to be there; whether his wife had tried to sideline him after his affair with Carmen O'Keefe, or whether there was something to him that kept him apart, made him the odd man out in the family, as Dermot, until he went mad, had never been.

It was months before Matthew could make up his mind on this, because he didn't see enough of Peter's father to judge. The first thing he decided was that when he was around, and only then, Jim Leary was the head of the family, in the sense that what he said went – without disobedience or even questioning. No doubt the heaviness of his hand had something to do with this. If the family was sitting around in the evening watching television, Jim might suddenly get up and say: 'Bloody rubbish. Can't hear myself think,' and turn it off. There was no appeal against this, and none of the children would attempt one. Bridget would say something like, 'It was pretty silly, wasn't it?' and the children would turn back to books or games, or, in the case of Matthew and Peter, the pile of stamp albums in the sideboard.

When Jim said he needed to 'hear himself think' what he meant, as often as not, was that he wanted to do his football pools, or study the racing columns of the *Sun* newspaper. Matthew gathered from Peter that his mother was kept on a rigid amount for all the household expenses, and the rest of his wage was inalienably Jim's, to spend as he liked on beer or small-time gambling. He didn't smoke, needing to keep fit for his job, but this didn't stop him enjoying a pint or two regularly at his local. His big pleasure was not drinking, but betting, and the nearest he came to being in a good humour was when he had had a win on a horse. Then he might, but more probably would not, add a 50p coin to his children's pocket money.

He regarded his elder son's stamp collecting as a form of gambling, and approved of it for that reason.

'One day you'll come up with a Penny Black,' he would say to Peter, 'in one of those job lots you get from the dealers. Then all our fortunes will be made.'

'Bloody fool,' said Peter privately to Matthew. 'The Penny Black's the only rare stamp he's heard of. If I did get hold of one I'd keep quiet about it till I was well away from *him*. I'd let my mother have her share, but I wouldn't let *him* get his hands on it.'

'Do you hate him?' Matthew asked naively.

'I despise him,' said Peter, not grandly, but stating a fact. 'He's nothing.'

It was perhaps this attitude in his children that led Bridget Leary to support her husband in his assertions of parental authority. He had irretrievably damaged his standing with his affair – or was it affairs? – but her bolstering of him was an attempt to glue the family structure together again. It was not reciprocated. When she was not around, her husband would speak of her with something like contempt. 'Your mother's in the grip of the priests,' he would say. 'By heck, what are they, to have silly women hanging on their every word?' Or he would characterize her as a blinkered person with no wider vision: 'Your mother's happy just grubbing along day by day,' he said to his daughter, Sally, in Matthew's hearing. 'Her eyes are on the ground, and she can't lift them to the horizon. Now *I'm* not like that.' What vision he saw in the skyscape he never revealed, but Matthew suspected it was a big win on the pools.

The remark about priests was in line with one of his constant themes, the scorn of religion. 'What's religion ever done for mankind, beyond setting them fighting one another?' he asked in one of his grander philosophical forays. 'Church? That's for women. They like men with no balls,' he would say if the question of churchgoing came up. That was a crudely-expressed version of Dermot Heenan's attitude, which Matthew had always found puzzling: if religion was *true*, it was true for all men as well as women, surely? 'If I want lectures on what I can and can't do,' was another version of the same thought, 'I wouldn't go to someone who's never done it in his life.'

This sneering at the church was part of a constant pattern of denigrating his wife and women in general. It was done on a bar-room level, but forceful and unremitting. Peter told Matthew it had been going on for as long as he could remember, but had got particularly bad since she had forced him to church and confession after his affair with Carmen O'Keefe.

'How did she do that?' Matthew asked.

'Sheer force of personality. Oh, she did threaten now and then to leave him, but he knew that if the family broke up it wouldn't be her doing. No, she just insisted – not nagging, but being firm. He's a bully, but he's got no staying power. In the end he caved in and went.'

But having caved in, he got his revenge in those mean little jabs at her religion and her attitude to life which had by now become a monotonous refrain. It was a happy little family when he was not there, edgy and watchful when he was. Peter said he couldn't wait to get out of it.

'After all, Mother doesn't need my protection,' he said. 'If I stayed, I'd want to take him on, and that would upset her more than anything.'

There was no way, Matthew had to admit eventually, that Jim Leary was ever going to talk about his affair with Carmen O'Keefe. Merely to approach the subject would be to invite an aggressive response, perhaps a violent one. And even if he had been other than the limited, very physical man that he was, how *could* one bring up the subject of an affair he had had with the father of a school friend? One day in the early spring of 1980 Matthew said to Peter: 'Aren't you going to be seventeen soon?'

'Yeah, in June. Why?'

'You can get a provisional driving licence then.'

'I know. I suppose I could. But driving doesn't grab me the way it does some kids.'

'You could get a car.'

'Buy one? Where would I find the money for a car?'

'Trade some stamps. You've got some quite valuable ones there, even if you don't have a Penny Black.'

'What would I do that for,' asked Peter, mystified, 'when I'm not really bothered about driving?'

'You could say that's what you're thinking of doing,' explained Matthew patiently. 'You don't have to do it . . . Kevin Holmes puts old bangers together and gets them on the road. The sort of car teenagers buy . . .'

Peter looked at him with a glance of calculation. Getting to talk to Kevin Holmes was one of the things they had often discussed.

'I suppose I could *pretend* to want a car.'

'Just bring up the subject sometime when your dad is there. And I am too.'

It was three weeks or so before that opportunity arose. It was one afternoon after school, when Bridget Leary was in Leeds buying summer clothes for Sally from a discount store. She had a sharp eye for what was simply shoddy, and what was slightly less so. She had to have, on the money her husband gave her for housekeeping. Jim was on nights, and had just got up after his sleep. He was in the living room poring over the racing pages, and Peter waited till he looked up from them to get a marking pencil before he said to Matthew: 'I think I'm going to start looking for a car.'

'A car?'

Jim Leary brightened up at once. Cars were important to him. There were cars he lusted after in his heart, in the way other men lusted after women, not so much for their bodies as for the symbolic standing they gave their escorts. He openly envied people who had such cars, and resented the fact that they were out of his reach. A car for Peter gave him something in common with his son. His wanting to own one gave him the signal that his son would soon be a man.

'Why not?' said Peter, apparently still absorbed with his stamps. 'I can get a provisional licence in June. There's boys at school who have licences already, and I could practise with them.'

'There's the little matter of money to pay for it.'

'I've got some pretty valuable stamps. I could trade them and get a car.'

'Have you, be God,' Jim whistled, now full of admiration. A hobby which turned out to be a moneymaker appealed to him.

'What you need is an old banger,' said Matthew. 'To practise in while you only have a provisional.'

'That's it — something to tinker with,' said Jim.

'There's that bloke in Stanningley gets old bangers on the road,' said Matthew. 'There's kids from school have got cars from him. Kevin Holmes.'

A shadow crossed Jim Leary's face. He was almost incapable of hiding his feelings, because he so seldom saw the need to.

'Oh yes? Isn't he from church?'

'Yes. The Christmas and Easter type, anyway.'

'I know the chap you mean,' said Jim, apparently casually. 'Drinks in the Golden Fleece in Stanningley. I've met him there after shifts. Garageman, is he?'

It was obvious he knew exactly who and what Kevin Holmes was. He was a very bad pretender.

'That's right. Dad always used to go to him because he was church,' lied Matthew, provoking an obvious sneer from Jim Leary. 'And he does up old bangers — or used to, anyway.'

'Hmm. I could ring him up and see if he still does.'

'That's an idea. Would you, Dad?'

It was uncharacteristic of Peter to ask his father to do anything. Jim Leary smelt no rat, however. He seemed pleased. Peter raised his eyebrows at Matthew as his father went into the hall. They heard him rather laboriously flicking through the Yellow Pages. Peter's brother Martin was in the room, and they enforced silence on him when they heard Jim dialling.

'Hello, is that Bradford Road Garage? Who am I speaking to? . . . Oh, well my name is Jim Leary.' When he got a response to this his voice lowered. 'Yes, well, I've heard about you an' all. Water under the bridge, eh? . . . No, I don't — I don't think anybody does.' Then the voice resumed its natural forcefulness. 'Reason I'm ringing, I've got a lad about to be seventeen and thinking about his first car. Makes you feel old, doesn't it? In no time I'll be over the hill . . . So you do do second-hand cars, do you? . . . The fact is, he's a bit of an expert on stamps, and he's going to trade some to get this car. That's the ticket, isn't it – know what you want and go after it. Chip off the old block.' Peter, in the living room, screwed up his face. 'But the truth is, he won't have a lot of money . . . Right . . . Right you are . . . So if I send him along you think you can fit him up . . . Well, I'll do that. We must get together some time. Talk over old . . . times. Right. Thanks very much. Goodbye.'

He came in rubbing his hands, in as good a humour as Matthew had ever seen.

'You've just to go along. Bradford Road Garage. He's got four or five things he thinks might suit you. I've a mind to come along myself . . .'

'Oh, that's all right, Dad. We'll only do a preliminary inspection. There's no point in actually buying a car before June, is there? That's when you'll be needed.'

The next day, walking home from school, was the first opportunity the boys had to talk the matter over.

'Your father's not very bright, is he?' Matthew said. 'He couldn't hide the fact he knew who Kevin Holmes was.'

'I've told you that. He's thick as pig shit. If it wasn't for my mother, he'd be a right mess.'

'Do you believe him when he says he's no more idea where Carmen is than anyone else?'

Peter frowned.

'I *think* so. I don't think he could have hidden it this long if he really knew. Like I say, he's thick.'

'Does he always ask who he's speaking to when he telephones?'

'What?' asked Peter, turning, with a puzzled look on his face.

'When the phone was answered he asked who he was speaking to. It's a bit unusual. Does he always do it?'

'Yes . . . Yes, he does, if it's not a friend or something.'

153

'Has he always done it?'

'No . . . But he has for some time now. Why?'

'It just didn't seem in character. It's the sort of thing a cautious person would do, and your dad's not cautious. It's as if he'd had a bad experience that's made him cautious.'

It was a clever comment, a bright piece of observation. But Matthew was not to find out for many years what it was that had made Jim Leary cautious on the telephone.

CHAPTER 16

Small Businessman

They caught the bus to Bradford Road, Stanningley, about a week later. They had talked over how best to get Kevin Holmes to talk, and had agreed that Peter was the one to do it, since he was on the verge of man's estate and about to enter, should he so wish, the world of beer-drinking and page-three-girl-fancying that his father, and presumably Kevin Holmes, inhabited. Matthew would drift around within earshot but outside the conversation. Matthew insisted that he had to be within earshot: knowing so much more than Peter Leary did, it was necessary for him to hear everything, in case the significance of something passed Peter by.

Matthew remembered roughly where the garage was, from his visit two or three years before with his father, when the family car had been (badly) serviced. It was in fact just off the Bradford Road, in a poor position, and it was little more than a ramshackle couple of sheds with petrol pumps in front of them and a big yard littered with cars in for repairs and cars waiting to be sold. The look of the cars in both categories was far from prestigious, even from a distance. Just outside the main shed door, a man in oily sweatshirt and dungaree trousers was bending over the exposed innards of one of them, exploring the mysteries of the combustion engine. All they could see of the man himself was a strip of flabby back merging into buttocks. Then he straightened up and they could see that he was a beefy man of middle height, running to seed and very dirty, with a pudgy face dominated by small, greedy eyes. If he had been photographed standing

155

there with his garage and wares around him he might have typified the sort of businessman destined to go under in the first Thatcher recession. He emitted the shimmer of failure. Matthew found he had very little memory of him from his earlier visit, but then he did not seem to be a memorable man.

'Carmen didn't go for class in her boyfriends,' commented Matthew. 'Or money either.'

'No, she didn't. What do you mean – that it's difficult to imagine how she finally netted a rich one?'

Matthew didn't quite mean that. In his mind he was wondering how anyone could believe she'd attracted a rich admirer, after the series of no-hopers she had been involved with. But he just nodded, and as Kevin Holmes bent back over the car, another thought occurred to him: if they were all, to a greater or lesser degree, no-hopers, were they chosen for something *else* Carmen was after, something for which she was willing to offer herself and her favours in return? Carmen was hard, blatant, voracious, but it was as difficult to see her *choosing* someone as dingy and unappetizing as Kevin Holmes as it was to see her managing to attract a genuinely rich man. If it was just sex she was after, couldn't she have pulled in much better specimens than the four men she had flaunted in her last year? And if it wasn't sex, what was it?

Peter looked at Matthew, who nodded. Then Peter led the way across the road.

'Mr Holmes? Kevin Holmes?'

'Kev,' said the man straightening up.

'Pete Leary,' said Peter.

'Matt,' said Matthew.

So there they were, all matey together. It was obvious that Holmes did not remember Matthew from his visit with his father. In any case, he largely ignored him, as not being at present in the car-buying class.

'I won't shake hands,' said Holmes, making a token dab at his hands with an oily rag which had been tucked into his trousers. 'No way you can do this job without getting dirty – not if you're going to do it properly. Wouldn't think I used

156

to be a white-collar worker, would you? Now, what sort of car had you in mind?'

'Well, just something that goes, really,' said Peter. 'And will keep going till I take my test.'

'Oh, you can be sure of that with anything you buy from me,' said Kevin Holmes expansively. 'I wouldn't do you down. And your dad and I are mates in a sort of way, so I'd make sure his son got a good deal.'

As he led the way over to one of the grisly collection of clapped-out vehicles at the far end of the yard, Matthew separated off from them and drifted over to two motorcycles a few feet away, pretending to examine them closely.

'Now, this really is a lovely little bus,' said Holmes, banging *tells* his palm on the hand-painted bonnet and producing a *its* cracked, tinny sound. 'L-reg, only one owner – a very careful *age.* lady indeed – and low mileage for its age.'

'Let's have a look under the bonnet,' said Peter, as if he would understand what he saw.

'Right you are,' said Holmes, lifting it up. It gave an arthritic creak. 'You're a lad who knows what he's about, I can see that . . . There now, lovely engine – I've been over it myself, practically renewed it. You'll get a nice turn of speed out of this car, if that's what you fancy.'

'The interior doesn't look too good,' said Peter, peering through the windows on the driver's side and viewing shabby and torn upholstery that wouldn't have reflected creditably on the one careful lady owner, if she had ever existed.

'I wouldn't have thought a lad like you would have bothered about the upholstery,' said Holmes, unfazed, as if giving a lesson in the truly manly view of such things. 'I can let you have a nice pair of seat-covers if you are. But the real selling point of this one is the engine. You'll find she's a really fine little motor for her age, with plenty of acceleration. Like I said, I wouldn't do you down because your dad and me's got a sort of bond between us.'

'Carmen O'Keefe, you mean,' said Peter, with a man-of-the-world smile. There was a moment's silence, then Holmes slapped him on the back and laughed.

'Well, I'll be blowed! Know about your dad's little fling, do you?'

Peter responded with an experienced-roué smile.

'I should do. They talked about it enough at church. And about you and her too.'

Holmes screwed up his piggy face.

'Oh Gawd – these women with religion! What a lot of cats they can be. Just because a man has a bit of fun . . .'

'Dad was married, of course. Were you?'

'Well, let's say I was and I wasn't. I was when I took up with Carmen and I wasn't by the time I finished with her. Pity that. A man needs a woman to go home to – someone to cook and do his darning for him. Trouble is, they want to own him exclusively. That's never been my line, and I don't suppose it's your dad's either. Well now, what do you say to this little job? I could let you have it for five hundred pounds.'

'Five hundred's a lot of stamps to unload. Could we look at something a bit cheaper?'

'Right you are.' Kevin Holmes heaved his dirty body off the bonnet and went over to another car that looked as if ten more miles would put paid to its travelling life forever.

'What's this one?'

'A Hillman Minx. Very good car in its time – family model, much loved. Now, I wouldn't say this was in the same class as the other, but it'll get you on the road and keep you there as long as you're a learner driver. I know because I've really worked my fingers to the bone on this little job . . .'

Peter let Kevin Holmes go through his unconvincing spiel for two or three more cars. Then he said:

'Well, I won't have any difficulty when the time comes. I promised my Dad he could come along and help me make the final choice.' He leered. 'You two'll have a lot in common.'

'Very funny,' said Holmes, unoffended. 'You're obviously quite a wit, young man.'

'Oh, I just meant generally. Because in a way you're the same type of chap – ordinary blokes. Not meaning to be insulting, naturally. But there is one thing I can't understand –'

'What's that?'

'Well, from what I hear, Carmen O'Keefe's boyfriends were mostly ordinary blokes like you and my dad. But if you believe the gossip at St Joseph's, suddenly she's swanned off with a rich admirer. I just wonder how she's suddenly managed to get her hooks into a moneybags.'

Kevin Holmes shook his head dubiously.

'*If* she did,' he said.

'You don't think so?'

'For a starter you don't want to believe all the gossip you hear at church. Has anybody seen her with this admirer? Does anybody know his name? I tell you, when I heard she'd gone my first thought was she was keeping out of the way of the police.'

Peter was genuinely surprised.

'The police? I never heard she was in any trouble with the police.'

Kevin Holmes began shuffling. It was obvious that he realized he'd said too much, perhaps made incautious by Peter's youth.

'Oh, it was just a thought.'

'But you must have had some idea what she might be in trouble with the police about.'

'Oh, she was always into something a bit dodgy, was Carmen.'

'What sort of dodgy things?'

Kevin Holmes drew himself up to his full height.

'Now just you give me a rest from these questions, young Leary. Anyone would think I was being grilled in a police station. I don't think being interested in your dad's old girl-friend is healthy, myself. Are you here to buy a car or are you not?'

At that point, Matthew concluded reluctantly that things were not going to progress much further on that particular line of inquiry. He strolled over to the pair.

'That's a marvellous lot of old motorbikes you've got there. I'm going to have one when I'm older.'

'Well, you come along to me when you are. I can see a whole line of customers from the Leary family.'

They didn't disabuse him of the notion that Matthew was a Leary. If he had asked his surname it would have made the connection to Carmen all too obvious.

'Did you work with cars when you had a white-collar job?' asked Matthew innocently.

'No – or only part of the time. I was an insurance assessor. It was a good job, but not for me. I wanted to get my hands dirty. I prefer this.'

Matthew's eyes went round the yard, an expression of interest and enthusiasm on his face. But he found it impossible to believe Kevin Holmes. In fact, he felt sure he had not left his job voluntarily. Had he just been made redundant, or had he, perhaps, been caught out in something crooked? The man's manner suggested that it was the latter. He did not inspire trust.

'Well now, if you two are not going to hand over the money and drive something off –'

'There's no way I could drive something off,' said Peter. 'Dad told you I wasn't seventeen yet. But we'll be back with my dad closer to my birthday. I expect these cars will be gone by then –'

'Not necessarily,' said Kevin Holmes quickly. 'You can never tell with used cars. And this new government seems to be driving the economy into the ground even quicker than the last lot did.'

'Anyway, you'll have something for me.'

'I will, I'm sure of that. Now, back to work.'

And he bent over the same old car – eternally tinkering, never putting to rights. Nobody else had come into the garage while they'd been talking, even for petrol. Both boys could recognize a business that was not going anywhere.

'Can we walk?' asked Matthew, when they were out of earshot. Peter grimaced.

'Walk home? It's a hell of a long way.'

'Well, start off walking. I want to get my thoughts in order.'

'Could you hear everything?'

'Pretty much.'

'It was interesting what he said about Carmen and the police.'

Matthew nodded vigorously. 'Yes, very. Pity he clammed up.'

'Do you think there's anything in it?'

'Maybe. The question is what she'd done that interested them.'

'But do you think that's why she took off?'

'She didn't take off. She was murdered.'

It was a decision taken suddenly, but led up to by weeks of uncertainty. He had to have someone who shared his secret. Annie was no longer interested, having re-made her safe nest. Peter was his friend – sensible, sympathetic, older, and already involved. Sharing the secret with him was a sort of friendship oath.

The word had stopped him in his tracks, and he stood looking at Matthew, his mouth open.

'*What?*' he said.

'She was murdered.'

'How do you know?'

'Annie and I found the body outside our kitchen window.'

Peter put his hands on Matthew's shoulders and looked into his eyes.

'You're having me on . . . Aren't you?'

'I'm not. It was June the sixteenth, the night she is supposed to have taken herself off.'

'But why didn't you tell the police?'

'They'd have found out about Dad's state and taken us into care. It could have been even worse: they might have thought that we'd killed her. She was getting very inquisitive about Dad, and why no one had seen him.'

'But . . . She was *killed*, was she?'

'Oh, yes – with a kitchen knife. I'd left the knife on the window ledge earlier in the day, which would have made it worse for us. But anyone could have done it.'

'But what did you do? Where's the body?'

'We took it to the little wood by Greatbuys supermarket and buried it there.'

'You dragged Carmen all that way? But she was a toughie – a dead weight.'

'No. We waited until midnight, and I drove. I don't know how I did it, but I did.'

Peter thought all this new and staggering information over. It was almost incredible to him that this young lad, three years younger than himself, should have done all this, and should now be telling him of it in such a matter-of-fact way, as if it was something only slightly out of the ordinary. He looked at Matthew with admiration as well as liking.

'So everyone thinks Carmen has gone off with a new fancy man, but you and Annie know that she hasn't because you found her body in your back garden?'

'Yes.'

'So someone else also came to your back garden that night, either with her or following her, and stabbed her?'

'I suppose so.'

'It must be, mustn't it? You've no idea who that might be?'

'None at all. Of course, I'd like to find out, but I wouldn't dob them in to the police. I reckon Carmen asked for it. Anyway we're just settling down as a family again, and I don't want us disturbed by the police barging in and going on about what we did that night, and why.'

'No, I can see that . . . Is my dad one of the suspects?'

'Well, all the old boyfriends are, except my dad: we'd have heard him, if he'd come downstairs. Anyway he's just not *there* enough to commit a murder.'

'Well, I must say you're a cool customer. And young Annie, too . . . Here's a 32 bus. Shall we get on it?'

Once on the bus, they said no more about Carmen's murder, except that Peter, thinking it all over, said: 'Thank you for telling me. I appreciate it.'

'I've wanted to for a long time.'

'Total discretion, anyway.'

'Total discretion.'

But when Peter got off the bus at his stop, Matthew thought: now three people know.

When Matthew got home, Rob and Grace, now permanently together as far as Rob's job would permit, were there on a visit, and boisterous games were going on all over the living room floor.

'You're late, Matthew,' said Auntie Connie. 'Where have you been?'

'Peter's thinking of buying an old car. We went to have a look at some. He'll be seventeen in June.'

'He'd do better to borrow ours. We've got no use for it, and leaving it idle's the worst thing for a car.'

Later, when Grace got up to make them all a cup of tea, Matthew followed her into the kitchen.

'You know all that insurance money for Carmen, Grace?'

'Yes?'

'Have you heard anything more about it?'

'Nothing beyond what we told you. They acknowledged that letter you wrote for Rob and asked him to let them know if she turned up, or if we found out where she is.'

'So it's just sitting there waiting for her?'

'Yes. Seems a waste, though I doubt she'd make good use of it.'

'What sort of woman was Carmen's mother?'

'A terrible old harridan, if you believe Rob. Kept a pub – had done all her life.'

'And how did she die?'

'Didn't you know? It was rather horrible. She died in a fire at her pub.'

CHAPTER 17

Connections

Fire.

As soon as the word was said Matthew knew that it gave him the key. He didn't think it through directly – he just nodded at Grace and began carrying the tea things through to the living room – but the word lodged there at the back of his mind, and the implications began burgeoning in moments of quiet, when he was walking alone, watching something boring on television, or, most of all, when he lay in his little bedroom, listening to Greg's even breathing, and engaged – as he so often had been in his young life – in thinking things through.

A fire at a pub. A fire for which a large sum of insurance money would be paid if the person to whom it should be paid could be found. Money that was now sitting around, waiting . . . Peter's father was a fireman. His own father had been a fireman before he was invalided out by the accident which had left him with a limp. Kevin Holmes had been an insurance assessor. Andy Patterson was an electrician. These men were not a heterogeneous collection of no-hopers. They were men who could help Carmen stage the sort of fire that would convince the accident investigators and the insurance company that it was accidental.

Carmen had been planning to murder her own mother. In fact she *had* murdered her, and successfully. Thinking it through, Matthew had no doubt she had had help of some kind from the man in the smallest bedroom along the landing, the man who had once been his father. The question of what kind of help, how much help, he pushed to the back of his mind.

'What kind of a woman was Carmen's mother?' he asked Auntie Connie one evening, when they were washing up in the kitchen. She shot him a glance.

'Pretty much the kind of woman you would expect,' she said.

'Like Carmen, you mean?'

Auntie Connie thought.

'In a way. I'd not want to speak ill of the dead, and in her style she was a clever woman, cleverer than Carmen, but I hated going near her. Early on in the marriage when I came to visit Rob and her, Carmen would say "You must come over and see Mum – she's so looking forward to meeting you again." I knew it wasn't true, and she never gave any signs of pleasure, but I'd consent to be driven over. I hated every moment of it.'

'Why?'

Auntie Connie paused in her vigorous scrubbing of the plates.

'She was a harridan. She could hide it from the customers, but it came out in private. She was as hard as nails, mad for money, scornful of anyone who wasn't. Oh, I didn't mind her sneering at me as a poor, dowdy country body with no go or ambition. But she sneered at Rob, too: "He's never going to make the big time, is he?" she would say. In fact, she liked to jeer at anyone who was ordinary, nice, gentle.'

'But you said she was clever.'

'In her way she was. A good businesswoman. And she knew her limitations. She was a presence in her pub: she put in an appearance, everyone respected her, but she wasn't there much. She knew she wasn't right for that kind of pub. So she had a nice young manager who really *was* the pub to its customers – friendly, warm, welcoming, as she could never be. And she was clever enough not to quarrel with him, and to give him his head.'

'Was it a pub like the Rover's Return?'

'No, it wasn't. It was rather up-market. It was – *is*, I should say, because a brewery bought it after the fire, and the young manager's just reopened it — it is in Tong Village, and they do a very good pub lunch. People came from miles around for it, because as well as the usual things — lasagna, steak and kidney, that sort of thing — they always had one unusual thing every day: coq au vin, fresh tuna, game pie. They had a very good chef, of course, and she was clever enough to pay him properly so as to keep him.'

'Was it an old pub?' said Matthew, thinking about accidents.

'Yes, it was. I'm not very good on history, but they used to say eighteenth-century. She'd managed to make it comfortable without losing the atmosphere. I can tell you, if it hadn't been for the woman herself, it was the sort of pub I'd be happy to have a drink in, and I'm not a pub person. She had a very nice sort of customer, served this real ale people go on about. Oh, the Fox and Garter was in lots of guides as a very special pub. Pity she was such a horrible woman!'

'She must have been cleverer than Carmen, if she could hide it so well.'

'Oh, she was. Carmen had been neglected as a child, and just went after what she wanted when she grew up. Her mother had had to work to get what she wanted, so she'd learnt things the hard way. She was disciplined, had control of herself. But it all came out in private. And once the customers had been sent on their way she drank like a fish.'

'Was this how she . . . died? Was she drunk?'

Auntie Connie nodded, confidently.

'She was asleep, and she'd been drinking heavily. I thought it might be a cigarette butt, because she chain-smoked once she was in her own quarters — never let the customers see her. But the fire people thought it was probably faulty wiring. The public parts had been redone, but the private bit was still as it had been — oh, back in the 'twenties, I think, when the electric light was put in. That's where they thought the fire started. So she'd have got her money out of the insurance people, though as it's turned out, there's no one to collect it.'

'Was it her insurance policy?'

'Yes. Took it out when she was convinced she had cancer. Doctor told her she hadn't, and she was medically inspected for the policy, but she was convinced. She always liked to do someone down if she could, and this was her way of doing the insurance company down. "You'll be nicely set up when I go," she said to Carmen. "You'll have the pub to sell and this as well. You can get yourself a real man, one who's a credit to you."'

Again it struck Matthew that Auntie Connie ought to have considered the unlikelihood of her daughter-in-law taking off and making no contact with the insurance company to ensure that she got her money. How long did she have to be missing before that thought was to strike anyone?

He said: 'All that money . . .'

'Oh, she's probably made contact with the insurance people by now,' said Auntie Connie. 'They wouldn't tell us, would they? Specially if she didn't want them to.'

So that's the way they're thinking, Matthew realized. It made sense, if you didn't know Carmen was dead.

Matthew brooded for some days on the new information he had got; in particular what it told him about his father, and his involvement with Carmen. He was at a point, now, when he regarded his father quite dispassionately, as a *fact*. There was no love and there was no anger. Love was in the distant past, when Dermot had been a real person. Anger was more recent, but it was difficult to stay angry with a blob. Dermot was like an animal who was not loved, but who was there, and had to have his needs catered for. Matthew loved Annie, loved his small brothers, but he had no one adult to love.

But there was his father's past, those mysterious last few months of sanity, and Matthew very much wanted to penetrate the secrets of those months, and perhaps uncover the seeds of his present state. A possibility occurred to him, and a means of checking it. The next day he announced that a project in history class meant he had to go into the reference library in Leeds. Auntie Connie agreed without a murmur: she was beginning to allow him quite a lot of freedom.

The lady behind the desk reacted quite impassively when Matthew asked for the *Yorkshire Evening Post* for the previous year. She asked which part of the year he was interested in, and eventually brought him copies of the first three months' issues which, collected in a stiff binder, came to a weighty and bulky mass which she helped him with to a table. Matthew already had a date in his mind around which to work: his mother had died on the thirtieth of January. He turned straight to that date, and immediately struck the gold he was looking for: on page three there was the headline: POPULAR PUBLICAN DIES IN FIRE.

The story, which he read through carefully, did not add greatly to his knowledge. 'Fire brigade called by a neighbour at 2 a.m. . . . fire had already got a hold . . . Mrs Rose Morley rushed to hospital, but it was clear she was already dead . . . had built up the Fox and Garter from a humble country pub to a well-thought-of hostelry with a discriminating and devoted clientele . . . a strong, no-nonsense personality very much respected by her customers . . . will be much missed in the Licensed Victuallers Association.'

There was nothing about the cause of the fire. That would come later. But in a way that was irrelevant. There had been no question about the cause of the fire − or, if there had, the investigators had eventually satisfied themselves that it was accidental. They had been wrong. Between her and her various lovers, Carmen had found a way of incinerating her mother that fooled the experts and left her collecting the insurance money and the price of the burnt-out pub. Or would have done if she had not met her comeuppance.

Matthew sat there in the dim, high-ceilinged Victorian library, trying to think the matter through. Carmen's mother had died the night before his own mother; probably, in fact, on the same day. When Carmen had appeared at Ellen Heenan's funeral she must have recently been to, or been about to go to, another funeral. The day his – Matthew's – mother had died, the news of Rose Morley's death had appeared in the evening newspaper.

Matthew tried to remember that day. They had just finished breakfast when his mother had said 'It's starting,' and had herself rung for the ambulance. She had been terrified that the industrial troubles of the Winter of Discontent would mean that no ambulance arrived, and she had an arrangement with Mrs Claydon up the road that she would drive her to hospital if necessary. However, she was assured an ambulance was on its way, and she sent Annie up the road to tell Mrs Claydon that she would not be needed. The ambulance had arrived in under a quarter of an hour, and the children had been left to watch and wait.

Where had Dermot been? Not in the house – but he'd been in the house overnight. That didn't tell one anything, of course. The fire could have been started by some sort of device. Or Carmen could have got into her mother's quarters at the pub and started it without Dermot's help. His father had had an early breakfast, as was his wont when he was in work, which he had not broken himself of when out of work. Then he had gone off, as he so often did, going round building sites looking for work, and calling in at the Job Centre. That was it. Before the ambulance came, his mother had rung the Bramley Job Centre and asked that a message be given her husband if he called in that she had been taken to the hospital.

It was late afternoon by the time Dermot was driven home. Plenty of time for him to have seen the *Yorkshire Evening Post* at the hospital, and to have been struck by the double blow. Because the more he thought about it, the less Matthew could see his father as any sort of prime mover in Rose Morley's death. Weak, yes; stupid, yes; wicked, no. He would not – *surely* he would not – have actively participated in the taking of his lover's mother's life.

And in fact there was a sort of proof that he had not in the result. He had seen the *Post*, seen the report of Mrs Morley's death, and realized that – unwittingly but foolishly –

he had been one of the agents of her death. It was that, combined with the death of his wife and baby, that had driven him mad with grief and guilt. To his simple mind it seemed like an instant judgement.

Matthew's mind strayed to the earlier stages of Dermot's affair with Carmen. With the other men, there had been a stage at which sex began to be mixed up with questions that caused them unease, and eventually led them to hot-foot it out of the relationship: those questions must have involved how to cause death without arousing the suspicions of fire officers and accident investigators. Either the other three men were brighter than Dermot Heenan, or Carmen had seen that she had to get subtler in her approach. What was certain was that Dermot had provided her with the sort of information or know-how she needed. Perhaps having provided it, he was immediately uneasy; fearful that it might be misused. When he read of Rose's death in a fire he was devastated. And the other news came immediately on top of it. That second blow had destroyed him.

Some days later, down the bottom of Peter's back garden, Matthew told his friend about Carmen's mother's death, and about his father's possible involvement in it.

'I don't think he *did* it, or even helped her to do it. That doesn't seem like my dad – even if he was madly passionate about her. But I think he provided her with the method of getting rid of her mother; the way to start a fire without rousing suspicion that it was started deliberately. She would have got it out of him because he was too stupid to realize what she was doing. But he must have wondered afterwards, and when he read of the fire while he was in the hospital, and then heard of Mum's death and the baby's, it drove him over the top.'

Peter considered this.

'If it did happen like that he could have hated the thought of Carmen, and what she used him for.'

'Maybe he does, if he can think at all. That's what we told Carmen when she came round.'

'He could have killed her.' Peter held up his hand as

Matthew began to protest. 'He may seem like a total mess, but he has the strength, and there could be some sane corner of his mind where he blames her for how he is.'

'How would he know she was there? He's shut away in that little room the whole time.'

'Before your Auntie Connie came he was alone in the house all the hours you were at school. He could have set it up himself – arranged an assignation with her.'

'He couldn't,' said Matthew obstinately. 'He could never have got downstairs and out of the house that night without our knowing. And you don't know our dad – you don't know the *way* he is mad. He's just a pathetic lump: before he went for treatment he wouldn't do anything without being persuaded or forced into it. Otherwise he just sat there. He's not all that different now. You're talking about him as if he was a normal man, or half a normal man. He's not.'

Peter left it at that. There was a sort of awkwardness about trying to persuade a friend that his father was a murderer.

That Sunday, Rob made one of his rare appearances at St Joseph's – Rob and Grace, in fact, though Grace said her being there was purely social, because she couldn't pretend she was a believer, let alone a Catholic. Auntie Connie was always trying to persuade Rob to go, so she was pleased, but Matthew suspected that one of the reasons for their being there was that Grace was pregnant and beginning to show. It was, on Rob's part, a sort of announcement. Everyone was surprisingly nice about it, and surprisingly relaxed ('It would have been a different matter if this was Ireland,' said Auntie Connie, though without explaining whether this made England a better or a worse place). Probably the congregation's acceptance of the situation sprang from their dislike of Carmen and their feeling that she had treated her husband abominably.

'You'll make a fine father,' said one of the women to Rob. The priest was friendly, and studiously took no notice of Grace's bulge.

Auntie Connie was now a valued member of the St Joseph's congregation – not too active in the weekday activities, because everyone recognized that, as an elderly woman with a brood of young children, she had her hands full. But she took the four of them to church every Sunday, her circle of friends increased, and she was respected as someone who had taken on in selfless fashion an onerous task. Her actual connection to the Heenan family was variously reported, but after a time it was simply accepted. Family ties in Ireland are notoriously intricate.

That Sunday, after Mass, everyone stood around in the sunlight in little groups. Jim Leary was also paying one of his rare visits to church, to sneer, and he and Peter stood joshing Rob and Grace. Some way off, Matthew was standing with Auntie Connie and her friend Mrs O'Hara. Every now and then he caught Auntie Connie looking over towards Grace and her bulge.

'You'd like Rob and Grace to be able to marry, wouldn't you?' he suddenly said.

Auntie Connie smiled at Mrs O'Hara, unembarrassed.

'Of course I would, Matthew. Any mother would.'

'Doesn't the law declare someone "presumed dead" after they've been missing a certain time?'

'Whatever the law may say, it's not what our Church says.'

'Does the Church say you have to know your wife is dead before you can marry again?'

'It's a lot more careful than the law will be, I know that. So it's impossible and not worth thinking about. I must make the best of it, and so must Rob and Grace.'

Suddenly, a moment after she had finished speaking, Auntie Connie jumped. It was something she had heard. Matthew looked up at her, then over to the other group nearby. The voice of Peter's father had floated over to them.

'So you're just starting out with a kid, while my Peter's about to buy his own car. I'd rather be in my shoes than yours, I must say.'

Matthew looked back again at Auntie Connie. Her face was now a mask.

'Is that Peter's father?' she asked, her voice not quite normal. Matthew nodded. She went forward to her son's little group.

'You're Peter's father, Matthew tells me. I'm his Auntie Connie. I heard you say Peter was about to buy a car. There's ours just sitting idle in the garage. He's welcome to have the use of that while he's learning.'

Matthew, watching, realized there was still something oddly unnatural in the way she spoke; even in the way she held herself. What was odder still, there was the same palpable unease under the habitual bravado of Peter's father.

'I say, that's a generous offer!' he said, with his usual eagerness to get something for nothing. 'Hear that, Peter? That would be even better than selling stamps to get one, wouldn't it?'

Matthew turned away from the scene, and made conversation with Mrs O'Hara on the first topic that came into his head.

'Auntie Connie doesn't quite know what to think about Rob and Grace and the baby. She thinks she ought to disapprove, but she can't.'

Mrs O'Hara smiled down at him.

'Well, that's natural, isn't it? We can't always follow the Church's teaching in our hearts, can we? I think everyone here understands. We all know what a horrible person Carmen was. Rob deserves a bit of happiness and a nice woman.'

Matthew thought for a moment, then said: 'Auntie Connie came round to yours the evening Carmen took off didn't she?'

'The evening after,' said Mrs O'Hara, in a matter-of-fact voice. 'We'd arranged it the previous Sunday. I had a bit of decorating to do, and I wanted her advice. I remember because we talked nothing but Carmen that evening. We didn't know she'd gone for good then, of course, but poor Connie was shocked she'd stayed out the night. She'd thought of ringing me up to say she couldn't come, but Rob told her it had happened before, and that shocked her still more. Poor Connie. It's a good job there's someone around with good, old-fashioned standards, that's what I say.'

Matthew, looking towards his 'aunt' and the other group of worshippers, felt something shut in his heart.

CHAPTER 18

Conclusions

They gathered in the hallway, and Jamie climbed the stairs softly to see that she was awake and wanted to see them. Greg had just arrived by taxi from the station, wearing his habitual worried expression. How Greg had become the worrier of the family Matthew never knew, for he had had the same sort of structured but carefree childhood as Jamie had. But it was easy to look into his face and see him in a few years' time, married and worrying about his mortgage, his children's education, what they should be allowed to watch on television, and for how long. Worry was already pinching at the features of his pleasant face. Perhaps he had understood, and felt, more at the time of their mother's death than anyone had realized.

Jamie sped back down stairs.

'She's awake, and I've put her to rights. She'd like to see us all together.'

They nodded, and started solemnly up the stairs. 'It's like the death of Mother all over again,' thought Annie. 'Only this time we're with her.' Jamie opened the bedroom door and ushered the rest in. It was odd how, since the others had left home, he had quite naturally become the master of the house. Auntie Connie lay there in a pretty pink bedjacket they all remembered her knitting, her face and upper body sadly thin and wasted, the eyes still sharp and interested.

'My, you're looking well, Annie,' she said, her voice sounding as thin as her body looked, but still with an Irish twang that was irresistible. 'Motherhood does agree with you.'

'It does. I always knew it would.'

She looked round at the little circle of faces, pride in her expression.

'Now don't look too solemn, all of you. You're together again, and that's rare, and I want to hear lots of laughter from downstairs. If I should drift away, what could be better than to go with the sound of your laughter in my ears?'

'Are you *sure*?' Greg asked, not needing to say more.

'Oh, yes. The doctor tells me it won't be long. And to tell you the truth, I feel it in my bones. I thank God I haven't had the pain that some cancer patients have. It's going to be quick and merciful.'

Annie went over to the bed and held her hand.

'You've been a good woman. You've done good. Everyone here knows that.'

'Oh, Annie, love, don't twist the knife! I've done all the silly and wicked things people do do, and then more. But when I look at you four, I do thank God. He only allowed me one child of my own. But then, late on, he gave me four more. And what a joy you've been to me.'

'We owe everything to you,' Annie said.

'No you don't. I couldn't be what your mother was –'

'You have!' said Jamie.

'You don't remember her, my lad. I can only say I've done my best. And I know that you'll all be all right. There's the joy of it. I know Annie will see that Jamie has a home, but even if she couldn't, I *know* that Jamie will be all right. It's in his face – and don't blush, my lad: it's a lovely face . . . So I've been a lucky woman.'

'We'll always remember you,' said Matthew, sticking to the literal truth.

'Oh, Matthew, what you and Annie must try to do is remember your mother, and honour her memory. The others are too young . . . Well now, you go off. We don't want a scene, do we? That's for books. They don't do any good. You go off and catch up with each other's news. I've said what I wanted to say. I've done my best by you, but the important thing is, you've all made me very happy, and it's that I remember now.'

'You've been –' Greg began.

'Now that's enough,' she said, raising a wasted hand. 'Be off with you. But I'd just like a few words with Matthew.'

Annie, rising from the bed and still holding her hand, looked at her reproachfully.

'Why with Matthew?'

'Don't be upset, Annie. Matthew and I have a bit of unfinished business – have had these many years. It would upset me too much telling you all. But he and I can discuss it quite calmly now, can't we, Matthew?'

'Oh, yes. Quite calmly,' said Matthew.

Auntie Connie watched them, feasting her eyes on them with love, until the door shut behind them. Then she turned to Matthew.

'Sit on my bed, will you, Matthew? I hope He pardons white lies, don't you? Because I've just told one or two. I know you can never love me like the others do, and I've understood that. But it's meant there's always been a strain between us, hasn't there?'

'Yes,' said Matthew. He added, to hide the bareness of it: 'Of course, being the eldest, I remember Mum the best.'

She shook her head vigorously.

'Oh Matthew, the time for lies and evasions is past. That wasn't the reason at all, was it?'

There was silence in the room.

'No,' said Matthew at last.

'No, of course it wasn't. I told lies to you, and you caught me out in my lies, and guessed the reason for them. Oh, there've been too many lies altogether in this business, and it's a wonder the good Lord let any good come out of it at all. It's always surprised me that no one asked any questions as to why I came and took over this house, and poor Dermot, and you children. You'd think the people at St Joseph's would have wondered.'

'I think they were so glad that someone did that they didn't *want* to ask questions,' said Matthew.

'Maybe you're right. I was a sort of gift horse, wasn't I? But it was a penance really, at the beginning. My punishment of myself.' Tears suddenly welled up in her eyes. 'Oh, you've no idea how I longed in those early months to be back in

Ireland, in my own home, with my own people! I'd forced myself into exile, and I was amid the alien corn. You children never knew how I wept! But He turned my punishment into the greatest joy of my life. I don't understand His ways, but I thank Him from the bottom of my heart.'

'Tell me about it,' said Matthew. 'The others will be wondering.'

She stirred in her bed.

'Sure they will, and you must tell them. In your own way, at a time of your choosing. Either now or after. It's difficult to know where to start. I've known I'd have to tell you before I went, but I've tried not to think about it. I've tried to write it down, but I'm not a writing person. I suppose it started when I came over on that last visit to Rob and Carmen, though things go back further – they always do, don't they?'

'You'd hated Carmen for a long time, hadn't you?'

'Oh years and years. Almost from the first time I met her. She poisoned my son's life, though he didn't realize it himself. I felt degraded being in the same house with her. But it wasn't that, Matthew.'

'Wasn't it? Are you sure?'

'Oh, yes.' Her mouth was set determinedly. He was not to think that. 'That would never have made me do what I did . . . I came over, and found that Rob had been delayed on the rig for a few days. That upset me, because I hated being alone with her. Her politeness as usual ran out after the first twenty-four hours. I tried to get out more, went to as many church things as possible, went to the Irish Club, though I never liked all the drinking that went on there. It was at the Irish Club that I heard about you.'

'About me? Or about us?'

'I heard talk about the Heenans. Talk was just beginning then: Carmen was asking questions, and you remember Greg let something slip at school. It was more than once, I think: you should have realized small children will talk. Mary O'Hara's little girl went home and told her mother that Greg's father was shut up in a little bedroom all day and never came out of it.'

'And she told you?'

'That's right. We just talked it over, gossiping, really, but I wasn't *involved* in any way. I'd known your mother a little and liked her, but that was the extent of it. But as we were talking, Carmen came over. "What's that about Dermot Heenan?" she asked — all sharp and tense. I could tell she was interested. More than that: I could tell she was *involved* in some way. And it wasn't difficult to guess what way that was. We told her about the rumours that were going round, and she snapped, "I've been round to see those kids and they're all right."'

'Did she claim to have seen Dad?'

'No, she didn't. It could have rebounded on her if he was found to be totally out of his mind. She said simply, "The kids say he's fine — just very busy." Even then the thought struck me that if he was very busy surely someone would have *seen* him. But then I'd never been much inclined to believe what Carmen said. I'd too much experience of her lies. I thought she was just making it up.'

'Actually, we had said something like that, to put her off the scent. What happened next?'

'Nothing for a bit. Rob came home, and that reined her in for a while. I was half expecting her to find some excuse to come round here, but I'd no evidence that she did.'

'If she did, it must have been just to spy. She didn't knock at the door. We'd told her Dad had forbidden us to let her in.'

'Whether she came or not, I know she was very interested. She didn't do it when I was around, but she was asking people for news of the Heenans, had they seen Dermot, and so on. This was reported back to me, because people hated Carmen, especially the women at St Joseph's. I was by now quite sure she had had an affair with poor Dermot. I was finding it difficult to be polite to her, and she hardly bothered to try with me.'

The voice faded away, very tired. Matthew squeezed her hand and let her take her time.

'The day she died . . . I told you lies about that.'

'Yes. Let's not go over that old ground.'

'We must, Matthew. I want it all straight . . . The arrangement with Mary O'Hara was for the night after, and she and

179

I had fixed it up days before. But the night she died Rob was to be out at a darts tournament, as you know, and I soon realized Carmen was taking the opportunity to go on the loose in some way or other. She said she'd be out for a bit that night, and I simply suspected she'd got a date with a man – maybe your dad, maybe someone else. Then it happened.'

'What?'

'It was early in the evening, about a quarter-to seven. Carmen was down in the garden, getting some clothes off the line. The phone rang, and I picked it up. When I'm in someone else's house I just say "Yes", because I haven't got their number off pat like I have my own. If I'd said the number, he probably would have realized it wasn't Carmen, but he didn't. He said, "How's the woman who incinerated her own mother?" . . . I know what people mean now when they say their blood turned to ice. Something started at the top of my spine and went all the way down. I just stood there paralysed. Eventually, I stuttered, "Who is that? What do you mean?" He must have realized then what he'd done, and he put the phone down.'

'He was blackmailing her.'

'Yes. Or getting ready to when the insurance money came through. I'll not say who it was –'

'I know, Auntie, I know. There's nothing to be done about that now.'

'No, of course not . . . Peter's a fine man. You made a good friend there. So much *good* has come out of this. I put the phone down and I just slumped in my chair thinking. The first thoughts were dreadful. I believed the voice absolutely. Carmen's mother had died in the fire in January, and I now knew she'd killed her for the insurance money. I was just horrified. I knew she was a horrible woman, but *that* . . .'

'Did you connect it with Dad?'

'I think at the back of my mind I was beginning to. Or at any rate to *wonder*. But mainly I started to speculate about what Carmen was going to do that night. She'd come in from the garden and gone up to change. She took an age, and when she came down around half-past eight, she just shouted, "I'm off", as she clumped through the hall and banged the front door. I went to the window and she wasn't dressed up – tarted up – hardly at all. Navy skirt and a yellow blouse – quite ordinary for her. *Not* meeting a man, then, I thought.'

'But you decided to follow her.'

'Yes. Her car was in dock, you see, so it was easy enough. As you know it's a fifteen or twenty minute walk to get here – a long walk for Carmen, but certainly not for me. I left it a minute or so, then began following her. She marched along, never looking back, so it wasn't difficult. When she got to the roundabout on the ring road I hung well back, but once she was across it, I could keep her in sight as she came up past the garage, and turned into Calverley Row. As soon as I came up and saw the name on the street, I knew what Carmen was interested in.'

'It had come up, I suppose, when people were talking about us?'

'Yes, it had: "Has anyone been round to Calverley Row?" – that kind of thing.'

'Was it dark by now?'

'No. Just the beginning of twilight. Carmen was walking near this house, but she was kind of irresolute. I disappeared into the garage and bought a torch, thinking it might come in useful after dark. When I came out, she was back on the main road and walking towards Calverley, but obviously just to kill time. I knew she'd be coming back. I came along Calverley Row, went into the field and waited as it got dark. As twilight fell, someone turned on the lights in the house here and pulled the curtains.'

'That would be Annie. She never left the curtains open when the lights were on. And eventually Carmen came back?'

'Yes. She was trying to walk softly, which didn't come easy to her. It was almost dark, and I was in the field just behind the garage of this house. She came quietly through the gate and up to the living room window. She went along it, looking for a chink in the curtains.'

'We always made sure there wasn't – once we knew she was spying on us.'

Auntie Connie nodded.

'Annie was a clever little housewife, even then. Carmen swore and went round the back. I came into the front garden and followed her round. When I got to the corner, she was bent down at the kitchen window. The curtains there were old, and had shrunk. There was a band at the bottom where she could see into the kitchen. There was no light on, but there was in the hall, so she knew she'd be able to see if anyone came to get anything. She was obviously hoping it would be Dermot, and she could see if the rumours were true. She was terrified, obviously, about what he might give away. That was behind everything she'd done since your mother's death. She had to know about your father, what frame of mind he was in, how he felt about her and what she'd done. Anyway, once in the back garden, and knowing she had a view into the house, she settled down to wait, and I did the same. After a time, there was movement inside the house, and lights went on upstairs.'

'That would be Annie putting Greg to bed.'

'I realize that now. Carmen strained forward to see, and I kept my eyes on her. Then it happened.'

'What?'

'I dropped my torch. It was plastic and didn't make any great clatter, but before I could even decide whether to run for it, Carmen was on top of me, had grabbed my arm, and was hauling me over to the kitchen window to see who it was. When she saw, she said, "Christ – I could kill you!" And I said: "Like you did your mother?"'

Matthew was leaning forward, caught by the terror of the scene.

'What happened?'

Auntie Connie shook her head, her face twisted at the memory of it.

'She went berserk. She threw me against the wall, her hands went to my throat and she began to throttle me. I don't know to this day whether she was in earnest, or whether it was just to frighten me. Probably she didn't know herself. But she had no self-control and I really do think – I'm not saying this to excuse myself – that she would have gone on.

I couldn't breathe, I felt I was bursting, and then, out of the corner of my eye, I saw that knife – a kitchen knife.'

'I'd been using it in the garden.'

'I suppose you could say it saved my life. My hands were free; I grabbed it and I stabbed her, first in the side, then when she cried out and started to fall, in the chest, again and again. If it started as self-defence, me saving my own life, it went on as . . . as something more. I wanted to kill her. I wanted to kill a woman who was so wicked she could have her own mother burnt to death. All my old hatred of her welled up with double force. I can't excuse myself, Matthew. It was murder.'

'Maybe that's not for us to judge, now.'

'Yes, it's God's mercy I'll be needing soon.'

'What did you do?'

'Carmen slumped to the ground, and I stood there for a moment, looking at what I had done. Then I just turned and ran. It was sheer panic. I'd *killed* someone. Me – a simple, homely body from County Clare – I'd *killed* someone. I ran down the path, out into the street, and started running back the way I'd come – wildly, feeling like screaming in my fear and panic. How I got across the ring road, I can't imagine. It's a miracle no one reported a madwoman. When I got back to Rob's house, it was quiet. He was still at the darts match. I went upstairs, got into my bed, and lay there, sobbing, shivering and thinking what to do.'

'Did you consider going to the police?'

'Yes. But I didn't do it. I'm a wicked, lying woman, I know that.'

'Perhaps you were meant for something else.'

She shook her head vigorously.

'I *decided* not to go to the police, Matthew. It wasn't God's work, it was mine. I couldn't face it – the shame, the shame for Rob, prison, what people at St Joseph's would say, what my neighbours back in Ireland would say. And once I'd decided not to go to the police, I had to be prepared to brazen it out.'

'I suppose you expected the police on Rob's doorstep the next morning?'

'I did. I got up, listened to the local news on the radio, and there was no mention of a woman's body being found. Rob came down to breakfast and said Carmen hadn't been home the previous night. He was concerned, but when I suggested he went to the police he laughed. Carmen wouldn't thank him for *that*, he said.'

'It wasn't the first time, was it?'

'No. He told me that later on. I pretended to be very shocked, but knowing what I knew about Carmen by then nothing could shock me. And I'd always had a fair idea what sort of life she led while Rob was away.'

'But what did you think as time went by and her body still didn't turn up?'

'Well, after a time, obviously, I couldn't go on thinking that nobody here had been round to the back garden. I thought your father must have discovered it and buried it. I'd worked out he probably had some connection with Rose Morley's death. I thought when he found the body, he was afraid the police would work out the link between him and Carmen if she was found in his garden, and somehow or other he'd got rid of her.'

'That makes sense.'

'Yes, it seemed to. So for a while I didn't believe the stories that were going round about him being out of his mind. Then I met Annie at the Irish Club, and something – I couldn't put my finger on it – aroused my suspicion. I think Annie's just not a good liar, thank the Lord.'

'I was always better,' said Matthew. 'But she convinced most people.'

'Perhaps there was something inside me that told me there was another possible explanation for the disappearance of Carmen's body. Eventually I *had* to be sure. I baked a cake and brought it round here. You were all playing noisily in the back garden. I came into the kitchen. There was a noise upstairs. Your father's door was open, and I think he gave some sort of groan or sob. I called up. There was no reply. I went up and – you know what I found. As soon as I saw him I knew he couldn't have got rid of Carmen's body. So I knew that you must have done it – probably you and Annie.

I decided at once that you had to be saved. That was how I saw it. You'd become trapped in a world of lies and deceit, and I had to restore your childhood to you. It was a penance: I would stop in England and give you normality again.'

The voice tailed away. She looked so tired she could fade into nothingness.

'The rest I know, don't I?' said Matthew.

'Yes, the rest you know. Do what you think best about it, Matthew. Your judgement is better than an ignorant old woman's. If you think it's better kept quiet, so be it. But remember Rob and Grace.'

'Yes, I'll remember them.'

'I'm sad I'll never see you married, with children of your own.'

Matthew shook his head.

'It's not something I've ever wanted . . . I'm thinking of entering the Church, Auntie.'

'The Church?'

'Studying for the priesthood, or whatever I'm up to doing. I'm not sure I have the brains for it, but I think I want to try.'

She looked at him, bewildered.

'But why, Matthew?'

'I don't know. It seems somehow . . . *logical*. Almost like a sort of thanks. I suppose that means thanks for you, thanks for being saved. It's difficult to explain. It seems what my whole life has been leading to.'

She shook her head.

'I'm a wicked woman to say it, and I never could if Father were here, but it seems like a waste.'

'If I thought that, I wouldn't want to go on living,' said Matthew, his mouth set in a determined line, as her own had been a minute or two before. 'Don't worry your head about it. Try to get some sleep.'

'I think I could now.'

Matthew bent over and kissed her.

'Sleep well. We should have talked about this long ago, Auntie.'

'I never could. You were always so *straight*. I almost

thought you'd have insisted I went and told the police.'

'That's nonsense about my being straight. I was the biggest liar of the lot.'

'For others. And I think you hate lies now.'

'Because I had too much of them all that while ago. Sleep now.'

'Remember – lots of laughter.'

But when he got outside the room he found the others assembled downstairs in the hall.

'What took you so long?' Greg asked, frowning. 'What was there to talk about?'

'Something I've known a long time but never really understood. I'll tell you about it later.'

'Does it affect us?'

'Not now.'

'We thought we ought to go and see Dad,' said Annie, with obvious reluctance. Matthew nodded.

'I suppose so.'

Jamie shuffled a bit, then turned.

'You've got to be prepared for a shock,' he said, as they started up the stairs. 'He's got a whole lot worse these last few months. There's no alternative to an institution now. Even if I wasn't going to live with Annie, I couldn't cope on my own.'

They paused outside the door. Then Jamie opened it and they confronted the horror of the little room.

Pictures of Perfection
Reginald Hill

High in the Mid-Yorkshire dales stands the pretty village of Enscombe, proud survivor of all that history has thrown at it. But now market forces mass at the gates and the old way of life seems to be changing fast. The Law can do little to stop the ever-growing crimes against tradition, but when a policeman goes missing DCI Pascoe gets worried. Andy Dalziel thinks he's overreacting until the normally phlegmatic Sergeant Wield shows signs of changing his first impressions of village life.

Over two eventful days a new pattern emerges, of lust and lying, of family feuds and ancient injuries, of frustrated desires and unbalanced minds. Finally, inevitably, everything comes to a bloody climax at the Squire's Reckoning, when the villagers gather each Lady Day to feast and pay old debts . . . and not even the presence of the Mid-Yorkshire CID trio can change the course of history . . .

'For suspense, ingenuity and sheer comic effrontery this takes the absolute, appetising biscuit' *Sunday Times*

ISBN 0 00 649011 5

A Coffin for Charley
Gwendoline Butler

Annie Briggs, whose evidence as a child was responsible for convicting two killers, feels a vague sense of unease and fears she is being watched. She then discovers that the murderers have been released and are living nearby. Annie dreads the revenge she knows will come.

But another killer is already walking the streets, cunning, inventive – almost a shape-changer. It looks as though the Second City of London is harbouring a serial killer – a killer the police think is called Charley.

Is Charley the one John Coffin, Chief Commander of London's Second City, must stop? And who is Charley . . . *what* is Charley?

'Gwendoline Butler writes detective novels that both in method and atmosphere are things apart . . . she achieves that real whodunit pull'   *The Times*

ISBN 0 00 647890 5

Less Than Kind
David Armstrong

1968, and Charles Somerville, son of impoverished landowner Philip Somerville, is on the run from drug dealers in the Welsh Borders.

In nearby Llantrisillio, newcomers James and Suzie find their sylvan idyll brutally and shockingly shattered by the voyeurism of a farming neighbour . . .

Also in Border country is Birmingham policeman John Munroe, liaising with Welsh colleagues on a routine inquiry. But a mysterious death in the area draws him inexorably into an investigation which is to uncover a tangle of dangerous passions running beneath the outwardly calm rural scene.

'Excellent characterization . . . skilful plot . . . Proof positive that Armstrong's fine debut novel last year was no fluke'   *Literary Review*

ISBN 0 00 649009 3

☐	CRACKDOWN Val McDermid	0 00 649008 5	£4.99
☐	THE RED SCREAM Mary Willis Walker	0 00 647861 1	£4.99
☐	NOBODY BELIEVES ME Molly Katz	0 00 647602 3	£4.99
☐	BAD CHEMISTRY Nora Kelly	0 00 647853 0	£4.99
☐	DOLL'S EYES Bari Wood	0 586 21862 9	£4.99

All these books are available from your local bookseller or can be ordered direct from the publishers.

To order direct just tick the titles you want and fill in the form below:

Name: _____

Address: _____

_____

Postcode: _____

Send to: HarperCollins Mail Order, Dept 8, HarperCollins *Publishers*, Westerhill Road, Bishopbriggs, Glasgow G64 2QT.

Please enclose a cheque or postal order or your authority to debit your Visa/Access account –

Credit card no: _____

Expiry date: _____

Signature: _____

– to the value of the cover price plus:

UK & BFPO: Add £1.00 for the first and 25p for each additional book ordered.

Overseas orders including Eire, please add £2.95 service charge.

Books will be sent by surface mail but quotes for airmail despatches will be given on request.

24 HOUR TELEPHONE ORDERING SERVICE FOR ACCESS/VISA CARDHOLDERS –
TEL: GLASGOW 041-772 2281 or LONDON 081-307 4052